FALSE
IMPRESSIONS

FALSE IMPRESSIONS

•

Ina Coggeshall

AVALON BOOKS
NEW YORK

PRINTED IN THE UNITED STATES OF AMERICA
ON ACID-FREE PAPER
BY HADDON CRAFTSMEN, BLOOMSBURG, PENNSYLVANIA

To my husband, Jack and our two daughters, Deborah and Kathryn.
As always, to Lynn Claussen for all her help.
A special thank you to my editor, Erin Cartwright and
assistant editor, Mira Son, for helping to make me a better writer.

Chapter One

"Let's hear it and don't leave anything out."

"Why don't I make some coffee." Jennifer McCallum, Bill Conlon's longtime girlfriend, walked away, trying to dodge the verbal blast that was sure to follow.

"Is this a one- or two-cup explanation?"

"I better make a whole pot."

"I was afraid of that." The Boston Police Lieutenant followed her to the kitchen of Gamble Coulhoon's apartment and slipped his large frame onto a high-backed stool at the breakfast bar next to the owner.

"Have you been demoted from homicide to robbery detail?" she asked as she measured the coffee into the filter.

"The dispatcher recognized your name on the 911 call and notified me and don't change the subject." He turned around, giving his attention to the room. "Whoever broke in here did a thorough job. This is no simple B&E, but then nothing is ever simple with you."

"Did anyone ever tell you that you have a suspicious nature?"

"It comes with the job."

"Jennifer and I had dinner together. We came back here for coffee and found the place like this," said Gamble, Jennifer's mentor and longtime family friend.

"I'm waiting for the whole explanation."

"It's my story, but I don't know where to begin," the older man continued. At seventy-eight, his past read like a popular espionage novel, full of intrigue and clandestine activities, many of which would never be made public. Recruited by the OSS, the forerunner of the CIA, he and Jennifer's father participated in too many capers to mention in detail.

"How about at the beginning."

"It's a little difficult to decide where that is, but I'll try. I'm going to have to go back quite a few years." He toyed with the cup as he waited for the coffee. "In 1946, when I was stationed with the Allies in Paris, hundreds of pieces of art stolen by the Germans were found hidden in the city. Since I was an art expert, they gave me the job to make sense of the whole mess. For once, the army assigned me to a task I knew something about.

"Along with a British major, Andrew Stone, and an American corporal, Sean Keegan, I began to catalogue, photograph and authenticate a cache of paintings, jewelry and sculpture found in the basement of a Paris bank."

"Who was in charge?"

"The Major was my immediate commanding officer, but I sent copies of my reports to the American High Command. I made two copies, along with the appropriate pictures, one for the Army and one for me. I thought it might be useful when I went back to civilian life. I did the actual catalogue work, the Major handled the logistics and the Corporal ran errands, drove the truck, the usual gofer jobs.

"It took about a year to complete. There were no great discoveries. The paintings were mostly Impressionists, but nothing spectacular, good, but no famous artists, at least not at the time.

"About a month before the project was completed, the Major and the Corporal disappeared. Their jeep was found in the Seine a few weeks later, but the bodies never surfaced. Before the collection could be moved to a safer place for storage, it was stolen."

"That could hardly have been a coincidence," said Jennifer.

"You're right. The Army looked into it, but couldn't prove anything."

"Where's all this going?" asked Conlon. It was late and he was tired.

"About a week ago, I was walking down Newbury Street when I noticed two small paintings in the window of a gallery. They struck a chord in my memory; I knew I'd seen them before. The frames, they were so unusual. Then it clicked in my brain. They were part of the collection I catalogued so long ago. Through the window, I could see a very attractive woman whom I assumed was a salesperson, so I stepped inside and asked about them. Her name is Elena something.

"She couldn't tell me very much, but it gave me a chance to examine them. In my estimation, they were part of the collection stolen more than fifty years ago. I asked to see the manager, but he wasn't available. His name is DeLacroix. I thanked her and said I would be back.

"As I was leaving, I passed an older man entering the gallery. Something about his manner seemed familiar. He was about my age, in his seventies, tall, shoulders slightly stooped, but he walked with authority, like a man used to giving orders. He was well dressed, most definitely the work of an English tailor. At first, I couldn't place him, but when I saw his eyes, I knew. It was Major Stone."

"Are you sure?"

"Positive. His eyes, they're a strange combination of gray and blue and his manner, it was he."

"Did he recognize you?"

"I've changed a lot, but, yes, he could have."

"And you think these things are related?"

"I don't believe in coincidences."

Conlon twisted his lips. He didn't either. "Does he know you made a second copy of the catalogue?"

"It was never a secret."

"Sounds as though he's got something to do with these paintings. If he's the same man, you could be in real danger. He must have gone to a lot of trouble to disappear. Add that to his involvement in what could be a multi-million-dollar stolen art ring, we have serious trouble. Give me a couple of days and I'll get back to you. Maybe I can come up with something. I'll check with Interpol. Meanwhile I think we should all get some sleep." Conlon checked his watch. "Come on, Jen, I'll walk you home."

"Thanks. Gamble, will you be all right?" she asked, reaching for her coat.

"It will take a lot more than a disrupted apartment to get the best of me. You go along home, my dear. All this can wait until tomorrow."

"Make a list of anything that's missing. Maybe we'll get lucky, but I doubt it," said Conlon. "Good night."

Jennifer kissed Gamble on the cheek and followed Conlon out the door.

"You know there's not much I can do," said Conlon, once they were outside the door. "There's no evidence that it's anything other than a simple break-in."

"Don't sell him short. He may be an old man, but his brain is still working on all eight cylinders."

"Do you believe all that stuff about his past?"

"It's all true and then some. I've heard stories from Dad about his cronies that would make your toenails curl. They were crazy. During the war, they did some things that are beyond belief. If Gamble thinks there's something to all this, then I'd take it seriously."

"I'm not questioning the old guy, but I need more. And that doesn't mean that you and your little band of amateur detectives should start poking their noses in places that could get them into trouble."

"My, my, aren't we defensive tonight. Come on, admit it, they're very effective and I'm proud of them."

"I'm not saying they don't do a good job, but one of these days, someone is going to get hurt. Please don't get them involved."

"I hear you loud and clear." They stopped in front of her building. "Coming in for coffee?"

"Can't. I have to be in court at nine. That means the office by six. Besides, you look tired. You've been pushing yourself too hard." He brushed a few wisps of hair from her face. "Get some sleep. I'll call you tomorrow. Maybe we can have dinner. Oh, one more thing. I never asked before. How did he get the name Gamble?"

"Rumor has it that when he was a young man, he would bet on everything. He was supposed to be a genius at picking the probability of things; how many days it would take the Allies to get to a point on the map, who would take command of certain strategic areas, that kind of thing. He even anticipated who would get to Berlin first and on what day. He made a lot of money on the Russians. Dad says he was uncanny."

"What you're saying is listen to the man."

"Exactly. Now go home." She gave him a long good-night kiss. "Love you and no midnight snacks."

She watched as he headed down the sidewalk to his car, then went inside. It was a five-story brownstone, purchased several years ago with money from a sizable trust fund endowed by her grandfather. She leased the basement apartment and the first two floors, but had the top three to herself. After living for years on Beacon Hill in the family home, she relished her own space.

Once inside, she got ready for bed, made some cocoa and climbed under the covers to watch the late news. Twenty minutes later, she was asleep.

Conlon drove to South Boston barely awake. Some liked the four-to-midnight shift, but he hated it. His body ached from the lack of sleep. He was forty-one years old, a lieutenant in Homicide, the most coveted division in the department. Well-known and respected by his peers, he was recognized as a man who got things done. The detectives under his command knew he could be counted on in a crunch. The term "a good man to watch your back" described him perfectly.

Traffic was light as he moved through the once close-knit blue-collar neighborhood that he called home. Now, thanks to the astronomical property values being placed on real estate, taxes were rising, forcing an unwelcome change.

He parked in front of a three-story white-framed building commonly referred to as a "three-decker," for it housed three separate families, one on each floor. In past years, they were usually related, but now, some of the buildings were condos with strangers living above each other. It wasn't the same.

He bought the house nearly ten years ago, just after he and Elinor were married. Now she was dead, the victim of a stray bullet fired during a robbery. Every time he unlocked his first-floor apartment, thoughts of her came flooding back. The pain had lessened, but the memory would always remain. He hoped the two young families that lived on the upper floors would fare better. But now, he had Jennifer. It was a new life.

He draped his jacket on the back of a kitchen chair and unbuckled his shoulder holster, placing it and the gun in the kitchen drawer next to the door. Visions of an ice-cold beer tripped through his mind, but Jennifer's constant lectures about his weight won out as he pulled a bottle of spring water from the refrigerator. A big man, his once-trim athletic build was now soft around the middle, but he was working on it. Tired as he was, he needed some time to unwind, and went into the living room to watch the news. Halfway into the late movie, he fell asleep.

The next morning Jennifer woke at her usual five A.M. Always too busy to put her laundry away, she chose some gray sweats from a pile stacked in the corner, splashed cold water on her face and brushed her teeth. She tied her running shoes, then took the stairs two at a time down to the kitchen. Putting a few dollars and the front door key in her sweatshirt pocket, she left the house, jogging a few blocks to Copley Square where her running group met in front of the main library.

She fell in line as they began their usual three-mile jaunt through the Common and Public Garden. The Park Service had outdone itself again, for the paths were lined with a blaze of spring color. Tulips, jon-quils, daffodils and hyacinths lined the walkways. She inhaled the early morning air, still fresh and clean, and stepped up her pace.

Breakfast at the deli followed. As she waited in line to pick up her order, Jennifer toyed with the idea of relating the events of the night before to her friends, but decided against it. There would be plenty of time to ask for help.

Once home, she showered and selected something appropriate from the closet. As she applied her make-up, she took a close look in the mirror. Conlon was right. She looked exhausted. Her usually healthy black hair was drab and in need of a trim. Tiny lines were evident around her lips and her lovely eyes, as they were often referred to, were dull and more red than blue.

At least the rest of her looked trim. Her stomach was still flat and her legs, still taut, and there didn't seem to be any flab showing. She could still slip into a size six. *At least something was holding up.* A day of pampering was in order. But when? That was the question. She had selected a black suit, but changed her mind, deciding on something with a little color, hoping it would make her look alive and pick up her spirits. She left her apartment still wondering how to cope with her latest problem.

The thought of fighting traffic was too much to con-tend with, so she rode the subway downtown to her office. Her secretary, Carol, was waiting, coffee in hand, along with a sheaf of pink message slips all waiting for her attention. She was the youngest full partner in one of Boston's most prominent law firms and chief counsel in their criminal division. Consid-ered one of the best defense attorneys in the city, she ran her department with total autonomy and few recriminations from her peers. At thirty-five, she was at the top of her profession.

Her office reflected her personality, conservative with a splash of style. The wallpaper, a pale cream stripe, had a soft sheen; the windows were covered with wooden blinds and the furniture, traditional cherry. The computer was state of the art, with a new thin monitor. The artwork, modern, but not trendy.

She returned the pressing phone calls and sorted through the case files piled on her credenza, but as the morning continued she found it more and more difficult to concentrate. Gamble and his problem loomed in the forefront of her mind. Her stomach knotted with the familiar feeling of trouble. This one had all the earmarks.

About eleven, the intercom buzzed. "Mr. Coulhoon is on two."

"Carol, he wants you to call him Gamble."

"I can't do that. He's so . . . so regal. I don't know. He may be Gamble to you, but he will always be Mr. Coulhoon to me."

"Morning," she said as she pressed the blinking button. "How did you sleep?"

"Like a baby. It will take a lot more than a simple intrusion of my privacy to distract me."

"All I could think of was what if you were there alone when they broke in and don't tell me you could handle yourself. These aren't the old days."

"You may be right, but I can't dwell on something I have no control over. Besides, they didn't get what they wanted."

"I hesitate to ask."

"If it is indeed the Major who is responsible for this, he's looking for a handwritten folder complete with pictures. He may not realize I've moved into the computer age."

"Would you care to enlighten me?"

"Not right now."

"Tell me about this Major Stone. Did you ever suspect he could mastermind a robbery of that magnitude and then disappear for so many years?"

"In the beginning, no. He seemed to be your typical British military type, honest, by the book, long on following the rules and short of imagination. He was career military, your typical aristocrat without portfolio, no title or money. But as the years passed, I concluded, the robbery was an inside job. It had to be him."

"Could he have done it alone?"

"No, he had help, probably Keegan and a few others. By the way, I stopped by the gallery on my way to the coffee bar this morning. The paintings are gone from the window."

"You didn't go inside, I hope."

"I did. They're not there. I did have a nice chat with the same charming young lady though. Knows little about art, but is certainly a thing of beauty."

"Men never change."

"I certainly hope not. I did learn one thing. The gallery is open tonight along with several others on the street. I think you and I should attend. Two art lovers out to enjoy a lovely spring evening and the local art."

"Conlon will kill us."

"How is he going to know?"

"He finds out everything. You're worse than a teenager trying to evade parental control, but you're on. I'm going to call Brian, just to be on the safe side. We may need him."

"I'll come by about seven. The cocktail set should be in full swing by then."

Jennifer hung up the phone and gazed out the window for a moment. Her view from the twenty-seventh floor afforded her a spectacular view of the city, one she seldom had time to enjoy. Her thoughts centered on Gamble. How she loved that dear man. She was three when her father first introduced them formally and it was love at first sight. He became the uncle every little girl dreamed of, someone who treated her like a princess, spoiled her constantly and became her closest confidant.

Instinctively, she toyed with the small gold charm depicting the scales of justice that hung from a heavy gold chain around her neck, a gift from him when she graduated from law school. It was her good-luck charm, a talisman. A shiver suddenly slid down her spine as she gave it one last tug.

She pushed the thoughts aside and pressed one of the memory buttons on the phone. Brian Foley, her private detective and one of her closest friends, answered in seconds.

"What does your day look like?"

"A few odds and ends. What's up?"

"Gamble's in trouble. Meet me for lunch in half an hour; Copley Square in front of the library. I'll supply the picnic." She hung up the phone and left the office, stopping at the coffee shop in the lobby to pick up some chicken salad, a corned-beef sandwich and two iced teas.

Brian was waiting in the small park that filled the center of the square. A former Boston Police homicide detective, he once served as her special investigator when she was an Assistant District Attorney for Suffolk County. When she entered private practice, he retired and went with her. She became the daughter he never had.

"This must be something good. I take it you don't want anyone around while you fill me in."

"You're still the best detective in the city."

"I wouldn't let Conlon hear you say that."

"I think he would agree."

They found an empty green bench under a tree and spread out so no one would join them. She passed him the sandwich along with his drink and filled him in on the events of the night before.

"Coulhoon," said Brian, "ought to write a book, but then most of his life is probably classified."

"You're right about that." She took a bite of her lunch and continued. "I need you tonight."

"What are you two up to?" He glanced as his sandwich. "Corned beef on rye, my favorite, with lots of mustard. You really must want something."

"I need you to watch my back. Gamble and I are going to the art gallery tonight. Every place on the street will be open. They'll be a lot of people so no one will pay much attention to us. The owner will be too busy sucking up to the money crowd."

"And what do you expect to find?"

"Maybe the paintings, I don't know, but we've got to start someplace."

"I'm not exactly the artsy type. I'll stick out like an Irishman in a Jewish temple."

"Put on a casual shirt, no tie and a jacket. Walk around and look interested. Half the people that go to these things don't have a clue as to what they're looking at."

"What time?"

"Gamble's coming by for me about seven. Get there a few minutes early and see if anyone takes a special interest in us when we make our entrance. We won't stay long."

"For the record, I don't like this."

"Noted. Finish your sandwich and stop worrying."

Chapter Two

It was shortly after seven. Jennifer, her hand resting on Gamble's arm, strolled down Newbury Street. As Boston's hot spot for trendy shopping and dining, the area teemed with pedestrians. The restaurant waiting lines spilled onto the sidewalks and the shops overflowed with customers. Business was brisk.

The beautiful woman, dressed in a short black dress of clinging jersey, hand-tooled silver hoop earrings, and high-heeled black sandals, along with her escort with his startling white hair, cashmere navy blazer and tan trousers, turned more than one head. A few knew their identities, but the buzz of overheard conversation identified a crowd who couldn't decide whether Gamble was her father or her sugar daddy. Most seemed to vote for the latter.

"So much for the unobtrusive entrance," she whispered. "Sugar daddy is my choice."

"I rather like that one myself. Shall I get you a drink?"

"Tonic water. Lots of ice, two limes. Make it look like the real thing. I need my wits about me. I've already spotted five smiling women ready to pounce on you the minute I leave your side, so behave yourself and keep your devilish charms under wraps." She gave him an affectionate pat on the arm and drifted away, pretending to admire the art.

As she moved along the wall, the room full of noisy pretentious people received her attention, instead of what was on display. The gallery looked the same as any other on the street. Stark white walls served as a backdrop for the artwork. The light from several rows of small spots in the ceiling filtered down on the paintings. The highly polished oak floor was devoid of carpet or color. The minimal look was still in vogue. Waiters skirted throughout the crowd carrying trays of small sandwiches, clever finger food and fresh vegetables. A bar in the far corner offered mineral water and white wine.

She spotted the three featured artists, each situated in a strategically prominent place, ready and willing to answer questions and promote a sale. She recognized a few guests, but spotted nothing that would look like it would help her on her quest.

Gamble was back at her side in a few moments. "I met Brian at the bar. Nothing so far," he said as he handed her a glass. "That must be DeLacroix, the manager, over there talking to that television reporter." He nodded his head to the right.

"What's her name? Linda, Linda Everston. DeLacroix looks like he could do without a few meals. He's, how shall I say it, pudgy. The suit does wonders though."

"My, don't we have a wicked tongue tonight."

"I'm an attorney, remember. The haircut must have set him back seventy-five dollars. The man likes the good life."

"Do you mean to tell me people actually pay that much to have their hair cut? Preposterous."

"You sound like Dad. Get with the program." She sipped her tonic water. "Enough small talk. Let's separate and meet by the hall leading to the restrooms. I'm assuming the office is in the back."

"What are you planning?"

"I need to get into that office."

"No, it's too dangerous. Have Brian do it."

"Maybe you're right. We'll go together. And keep your voice down."

"That's not what I meant and you know it."

"Don't worry. We'll be fine. You stand guard in the hall. If anyone comes, stop him or her. Ask a few questions, loudly, so we can hear you. Distract them. Use your famous charm so we can sneak out." She walked away before he could protest further and edged up to Brian standing near the bar.

"We're going into the office. Follow me down the back hall. Gamble's going to stand guard."

"I hope you know what you're doing. I can just see the headlines. Defense attorney busted with ex-Boston Police detective for B&E."

Jennifer moved away, slowly weaving through the crowd, stopping to smile and say hello to a few people she recognized. Ten minutes later, she found Brian standing in the shadows of the hallway.

"It's unlocked. I didn't even have a chance to try my new computerized pick. Takes all the fun out of it." He opened the door slowly and pulled her inside. They each took a penlight and began shining them around the room.

"I'll start with the desk," whispered Brian.

"I'll go there," she replied, pointing to the filing cabinet by the window. "Maybe we'll get lucky." She crossed the room and opened the top drawer. The gallery specialized in the moderns, so she began looking in the files for any mention of older works of art.

In the third drawer down, she spied a red folder marked "special clients" on the tab. She pulled it out and flipped through the contents. "I think I found something," she whispered.

"Well, there's nothing here." Brian moved to her side.

"Look. These are pictures of Impressionist paintings, nothing I recognize, but I think it's what they call 'in the school of' and several letters, sales slips and appraisals of authenticity." She looked around the room. "We need to make copies."

"There's a machine over there," said Brian, pointing to a large shadow across the room. A tiny green pinpoint from the "on" button could be seen glowing in the dark. "We're in luck, the thing's still on." He took the file. "Go outside and keep watch with Gamble. I'll take care of this and put the original back."

Jennifer slowly opened the door and joined Gamble at the end of the hall. "We found something," she said quietly. "Brian's making copies. He needs about five minutes."

Two women passed them on the way to the ladies' room. Then a young attractive woman walked toward them. "It's that lovely young sales assistant who was here the day I came in," said Gamble.

"I hate her. Not an ounce of fat on her anywhere."

The woman called out as she approached them. "Have you come back for another look?" she asked, displaying a perfect set of capped white teeth.

"How could I resist such a wonderful array of realism. Perhaps you could answer a question or two for me," he said, gently squeezing her arm as he guided her away from the hall and back into the main room. Jennifer breathed a sigh and returned to her vigil.

She turned back toward the office just as Brian was closing the door. His hands were empty.

"Where are the copies?"

"In my pocket. You didn't expect me to walk out with a fistful of papers, did you?"

"No, of course not. I'm nervous. Nocturnal break-ins are not exactly my specialty."

"Let's go before something happens." Suddenly Brian grabbed her arm. "Wait. Look by the door. If I'm not mistaken, the Major has just joined the party."

"You mean the tall man with the gray hair standing at the bar?"

"That's the one. He fits Gamble's description. Got that military look, even at his age." Brian looked around the room. "Where's Gamble?"

"Behind him, near the door. Let's go. I want him out of here before the Major spots him."

Separating, the two headed for the entrance. Jennifer brushed Gamble's arm in passing. "Mission accomplished. Let's get out of here."

Conlon was waiting for them when they reached Jennifer's address. "What have you three been up to?" he asked. "No good, I bet."

"What makes you think that?" Jennifer, trying to keep a straight face, avoided his eyes.

"Why don't we go inside and you can tell me all about it."

Jennifer unlocked the door and the three men followed her up the stairs. Once inside, she turned on the light, opened the French doors leading to her balcony and motioned them outside. "I'll make something to eat. Brian, fill him in. He'll find out sooner or later."

Taking the papers from his pocket, Brian spread them on the glass-topped table. "We found these in the gallery office."

"Found?"

"We stumbled on them. Let's leave it at that."

"Breaking and entering is a felony."

"The gallery office was unlocked," Jennifer called.

"Your twist on the word doesn't change anything; it's still a crime."

"So, we took a few liberties," said Brian. "Let's check out the stuff."

"This particular gallery deals in modern art and what I see listed on these pages doesn't fall under that category." Gamble studied the papers a page at a time. "The pictures are blurred, but I'm sure I can compare them to my own."

"Who runs the place?" asked Conlon.

"His last name is DeLacroix," offered Gamble. "Supposedly, the owners have a gallery in Paris. That's all I know, but I'll have my sources in the art world check."

"Interpol should be able to help us out. Their art experts have fairly up-to-date info," said Conlon.

Gamble returned his attention to the files. "These seem to be sales records, mostly paintings to various people and museums throughout the world. Some date back several years. There's no mention of the artists or previous owners, just descriptions and some numbers. It may be a code."

He separated the papers into piles. "The paintings are mostly Impressionists, but there is mention of a few pieces of jewelry and some sculpture."

"What's your take on all this?" Conlon tapped the files.

"I'm not sure yet. I need more information. Once I do the comparison, I'll have a better idea."

Jennifer returned with a plate of sandwiches and a pot of coffee. As she poured, each man eagerly bit into the roast beef and cheese. "I didn't know I was such a good cook." Her reputation for not knowing her way around the kitchen was well known.

"What do we do next?" Gamble tidied the papers.

"Nothing!" said Conlon. "Look, don't do anything stupid. If what you suspect is true, these men have a lot to lose. Let's see what Interpol comes up with first. You three have done enough damage for one night."

"I'll confine myself to research," replied Gamble. "I'm not getting any younger. I know my limitations."

"Why do I not believe that." Conlon shook his head, afraid to think about what was to come.

Gamble slowly got up from his chair. "Brian, why don't you walk an old man home. I'm sure these young people would like a little time alone."

"Right." Brian nodded to Conlon and gave Jennifer a kiss on the cheek. "I'll see you tomorrow." The two men let themselves out.

Conlon rubbed the back of his neck, then poured them both another cup of coffee. "Not only do I have a major international stolen art ring working in my city, I've got an over-the-hill spook to worry about. You've got to control him, Jen. He could get into real trouble. He lives by a code of ethics that doesn't exist anymore."

"I'll see what I can do, but he's got a mind of his own."

"He was here, I'm telling you. I saw him," shouted Sean Keegan. Major Stone and André DeLacroix, the gallery manager, sat in the gallery office watching him pace up and down the room. A slightly built man with a receding hairline of dyed dark brown hair, he had an overabundance of energy and looked sixty instead of seventy-four.

"Who was with him?" asked Stone.

"That nosy woman lawyer, the one who has her picture in the paper all the time. Didn't you see them? The walked right past you when they came in."

"No. How long did they stay?" asked DeLacroix.

"About an hour, but that's not the point. What were they doing here?"

"Maybe they were looking at the art." Stone sipped the last of his drink. "They say she's very wealthy."

"I don't like it." DeLacroix nervously crumpled the cocktail napkin with his fat fingers and wiped the sweat from his brow.

"What about Harrington, our new partner. What if he finds out? He's got eyes everywhere and he's dangerous. He's not going to like this." Keegan paced even faster. "We gotta do somethin'."

The Major got to his feet. "Calm down, both of you and don't jump to conclusions. For years, everything has run smoothly because we carefully planned every move and never panicked. They don't know anything and can only be guessing at this point." He looked at both of them. "I don't want any violence. Any rash action could open us up to a great deal of unwanted attention. We'll have to wait and see how it plays out."

Chapter Three

Gamble Coulhoon was the survivor of an extraordinary life. A graduate of an Ivy League college, he once envisioned an innovative career in the art world as an expert restorer and appraiser of Impressionist paintings. World War Two forced an abrupt change.

Fluency in several languages and family connections worldwide made him a perfect target for special projects recruitment. When the Allies discovered hundreds of pieces of art confiscated by the Germans in the cellar of a Paris bank, they delegated him to identify and catalogue it all, and hopefully discover the rightful owners. He spent three years in the capital city, attempting to untangle the hopeless problem of ownership.

Before he could return to the civilian world, the OSS, soon to become the CIA, made him an offer he couldn't refuse, ensuring that the next thirty-five years would be immersed in exciting, often dangerous assignments. Now retired, he assumed it was all behind him, but the sudden resurrection of a supposed dead man had his juices flowing again.

Until this moment, Gamble had forgotten how much he missed the intrigue and danger that filled nearly all his adult life. Involving Jennifer made him uneasy, but the rest was a temptation. The mystery had grabbed him, taken hold of his imagination and wasn't about to let go.

But all that had to wait. Finishing his usual early-morning coffee and donut at his favorite neighborhood coffee bar, he headed for the subway station and the short ride to one of the local universities where he taught two art restoration classes in their Masters program.

He joined the throng of morning commuters as they converged down the stairs and took his place next to the tracks below the streets of the city. As he waited, he read the morning paper, paying little attention to those around him. Engrossed in the editorial page, he barely listened to the reverberations of the green trolley as it rumbled through the tunnel toward his stop.

Suddenly, as the screech of brakes filled the air and the crowd tensed to embark, he felt a nudge, a small one at first, then another, this time with considerable strength, pushing him forward toward the tracks, directly in front of the path of the oncoming car. Someone was trying to kill him. Only his quick reflexes, excellent balance and years of experience in dangerous situations saved him from certain death.

Automatically, he rose on his toes and, crouching slightly, turned quickly, hoping to grab his assailant, only to find a sea of innocuous faces waiting to board the car. He was too late. As the folding doors squeaked open, Gamble creased the paper and joined the others, grasping the metal handrail harder than usual as he mounted the steps. His arm shook and a trickle of sweat began its journey down the back of his neck. *You're getting old,* he thought. *You let your guard down. Well, not anymore. Whoever you are, it won't be so easy the next time.*

He spent the next three hours with his students, but his mind kept wandering back to the mystery at hand. Dismissing his second class early, he went directly to his office and phoned an old friend and colleague from the old days, a man known to dispense sound advice with an extraordinary ability to ferret out the most subtle of schemes.

"Marko, my friend, it's good to hear your voice."

"Gamble, you old devil. What are you up to?"

"Have lunch with me. I have an interesting proposition for you."

"I hope you're calling to take me away from this boring life of reading and quiet nights slumped in front of the idiot box."

"I'm certainly going to try. Meet me at the pub near City Hall. You remember it, I'm sure."

"That place will be full of camera-toting tourists, all searching for our country's roots, and high-powered businessmen padding their expense accounts."

"Just what I had in mind. Quarter to twelve so we can get a table."

"Got it. Sounds like something big."

"If my hunch is correct, my friend, it is. I guarantee it will be worth your while." As he was about to leave, the phone rang. Frowning, he reluctantly picked up the receiver. "Jennifer, how nice to hear from you."

"When you use that phony British accent on me, I know you're up to no good. Give."

"You are your father's daughter."

"I'm the product of two exceptional teachers. Remember that when you try to pull the wool over my eyes."

"I concede to your remarkable observations. Meet me at that pub near City Hall, the one with the outside seating, twelve o'clock."

"That place will be jammed."

"Exactly."

"Are we practicing clandestine meetings in public places?"

"A bit melodramatic, but yes."

"You're on. I may be few minutes late."

He hung up the phone and made a fast exit before he could be detained again.

Gamble was already seated when Jennifer arrived. She knew most of his friends, but didn't recognize the man sitting opposite him at the table. He was about the same age as her old friend, but not as tall. Dark wavy hair, at least what was left of it, framed his deeply tanned angular face. Slightly tinted glasses hid the color of his eyes. A navy blazer and starched white shirt open at the neck gave him a sophisticated European air.

"Sorry I'm late," she said as she slipped onto the chair next to Gamble.

"Jennifer, this is Marko Bertoni, a colleague of mine and your father's from the old days." He could see Bertoni raise an eyebrow. "This young lady is Brand McCallum's daughter. I have very few secrets from her."

Jennifer extended her hand. "Mr. Bertoni, a pleasure."

"The pleasure is all mine, my dear." He smiled and returned the firm handshake. "Have we met before? You look familiar."

"I don't think so. My picture's been in the paper a few times. That might be it."

"She's a defense attorney, quite famous, I might add," said Gamble.

"Your father is an admirable man. It was my pleasure to have known him many years ago. I take it he's well?"

"He's recovering from a recent stroke, but yes, he's in good spirits. I'll give him your regards. Did you work with him?"

"I was under his command during and after the war. Italian is my second language and my family had many ties to the old country that proved useful many times."

Jennifer nodded. She knew not to probe any further. Clandestine life was just that, a secret. "Enough small talk, gentlemen. What's going on? A simple lunch is obviously not an option for you two. Besides, it's written all over your face."

"We must be slipping, Marko."

"Maybe you could fool the average person, but I know this man too well."

The waiter appeared to take their order. Gamble waited until he was well out of earshot before he told them about the attempt on his life earlier in the day. "We've got someone worried," he added.

"Pulling a stunt like that on an old pro like you. I'd say they're desperate," said Marko.

"I hate to remind you, my old friend, we're no spring chickens."

"We're not senile, either. The bones may creak a little, but the mind hasn't gone south yet. From what I remember of your Major Stone, it doesn't strike me as his style. He wasn't especially clever and definitely not theatrical or violent. He even hated guns. I can't believe he masterminded this attempt on your life."

Bertoni settled back in his chair. A slight smile curled the end of his lips. "Tell me what you've got up your sleeve."

"The gallery has ties to Paris. I need some in-depth background. Who, what, you know the drill."

"Do you think he's using someone from the old days?"

"The Major had free rein during the war. He could have used the investigation as a cover to recruit members to set up his organization. It appears to be a well-preserved operation. A careful thorough person is behind this."

"You think he's in charge?"

"He didn't know anything about smuggling. Of course, he must have learned it by now, but my guess, someone else is calling the shots."

"All this was planned a long time ago," said Jennifer. "Most of them must be dead by now."

"True, but there's always family members and new recruits. This operation was planned for the long haul, not for a quick profit. It's probably been tweaked to keep up with the times."

"I'll use some of my old contacts. Some are gone, of course, but the network is still intact. What else do you need?" asked Marko.

"Jennifer, I didn't tell Conlon, but over the years, as many as a hundred pieces have been auctioned on the open market. I've kept track of the public sales, but I'm sure many others have been sold illegally to private collectors. I've recorded everything on disk. One copy is in my safe deposit box and now you're going to have one." He handed her a small white envelope. "Put it in a safe place."

"That's what you alluded to on the phone this morning." She put the envelope in her bag.

"With concentration and practice, the computer's not difficult to master."

"I would never question your ability to do anything."

"It's going to be difficult, but I think we can trace a lot of them. You'd be amazed what a picture of Ben Franklin can produce."

"Please be careful. I don't want to read about either of you in the morning headlines."

"One more thing. Two men followed me when I left the university, but I managed to lose them. I don't know what they're up to, but they'll be back. Next time, I may not be so lucky."

The waiter returned with their orders. Gamble patted her on the hand. "Enough of business. Now we can enjoy our lunch."

Two hours later, Jennifer was back at her office. She smiled at the thought of her two luncheon companions. It reminded her of her childhood. Men coming to the house at all hours, frantic phone calls, things discussed in hushed tones.

She wasn't alive in the forties, but the Cold War remained a constant threat as she grew up. At the time, Brand McCallum's activities remained a secret, but as she grew older, the pieces came together. When her father retired, he began revealing many of his escapades. She heard about his assignments during the war, his activities in the ensuing years and his many unsung contributions to the free world. His career had been varied: special consultant to the president, successful attorney, an appointment to the federal judiciary, a man well respected for his fairness and integrity. Now she needed a second opinion and knew just where to go.

Leaving her office early, Jennifer walked the few blocks to her father's home in Louisburg Square on

Beacon Hill, the posh enclave of the rich, nestled on a hill behind the State House. She shopped the antique store windows that lined Charles Street, paid cash for a bunch of colorful flowers from the corner market, then began the short trudge up Mount Vernon Street.

When she reached the top, she stopped to admire the familiar tree-filled park surrounded on three sides by some of the most beautifully restored townhomes in the city. Enclosed by a wrought-iron fence, the small space of green with its benches provided a place for the residents to enjoy the afternoon breeze. The sight lifted her spirits.

Suddenly, she experienced a strange feeling. It was as though someone was watching her. She remembered the conversation with Gamble earlier in the day. A coincidence, perhaps, but she didn't believe it, another lesson from her father. Turning around slowly, she scanned the streets. No one, but the impression remained.

Passing the black lacquered front door with the elegant brass knocker, she walked around back and entered through the kitchen on the lower level. She found Maribel, the longtime housekeeper, seated at a large harvest table by the window, enjoying her afternoon cup of tea. She was a tiny slip of a woman. Her short graying hair was pulled back to reveal a round pleasant face beaming at the sight of her visitor.

Jennifer put the flowers on the counter and rummaged in a cabinet for a vase. She made an attempt at an arrangement and brought it to the table. "For you," she pronounced and proceeded to find a cup and fill it with tea. "And how is the patient?" she asked as she pulled out a chair.

"He's glad to be home," Maribel replied, smiling at the small gift. "Six months at that nursing home was almost more than he could bear. Was no picnic for me either, I'll tell you that! All that running back and forth, sneaking sweets and homemade bread into his room. Can't blame him though. The food in that place was a disgrace. It's no wonder he's so thin."

"Is he awake?"

"He's out on the terrace enjoying the afternoon sun. He'll be so glad to see you."

"Enjoy the flowers." She gave Maribel a pat on the arm and climbed the stairs to the walnut-paneled hall and out to the small brick patio jutting from the side of the house. She paused at the doorway for a moment, watching her father. Maribel was right. He was thin. The stroke had taken its toll. A man whose escapades rivaled those of Gamble Coulhoon, the ruling patriarch of one of Boston's leading families, representing more than two hundred years of accepted power, was now an old man, weak and frail. It frightened her. She wondered if she should bother him with this problem.

Suddenly he stirred in his chair and opened his eyes. "Jennifer, how nice of you to come. You're not playing hooky, are you?"

"I decided to take the afternoon off to visit my favorite person." She kissed him on the cheek and grasped his hand. For a fleeting second, she remembered the strength it once conveyed. Now it was thin and slightly limp. She squeezed it gently and pulled a chair next to his.

"You've got that look." His voice was still clear and distinct. The stroke had mercifully spared his mind and ability to speak.

"What look?"

"The one that appears when you have a difficult problem."

"Right again, as usual."

"This old body may be failing, but my mind still has a long way to go."

"Seems as though I heard that same sentiment just a few hours ago. I need your input on something."

"A difficult case?"

"Not exactly. Gamble and I had lunch today and I met an old friend of yours, Marko Bertoni."

"Marko. I haven't seen him in years. He and Gamble made quite a pair. They were two of my best agents back in the fifties. What are those two conspiring and how does it involve you?"

She spent the next few minutes describing what had transpired earlier in the day, leaving nothing out.

"So the Major's alive. I remember the case. We always knew there was some connection between the disappearance and the theft, but could never prove it. For years we tried to find some trace of them, but came up with nothing."

"Gamble says that over the years a lot of the pictures have surfaced on the open market. He's sure others were sold in the black market."

"That's true. We tried to trace them, but the art world is mysterious. They keep things close to the vest. After the war, there was so much confusion over ownership that the authorities all but gave up. We didn't have computers in those days and depended on hand-written documents, most of them badly decomposed, destroyed or conveniently misplaced. Even the museums had problems proving ownership. It's not much better today."

"Someone tried to push Gamble in front of the Green Line car at Copley Station this morning. I think he's in real danger."

"What does Conlon think?"

"He doesn't know yet. I'm meeting him for dinner."

"Give me a little time to think about this," he said slowly.

She could tell by his eyes that his strength was waning. "I've got to go. I'll call you tomorrow."

He nodded, barely keeping his eyes open as she gently hugged him and wiped the tears from her eyes.

Once outside, she began the short walk to meet Conlon for dinner in the North End, an area known for its abundance of excellent Italian restaurants. Her route took her through Faneuil Hall, the historic marketplace in the heart of the city, now a restored vibrant retail area filled with shops and eateries of every nature. It bustled with customers, tourists and natives alike, enjoying the ambiance of a successful restoration project.

Moving through the crowd, she experienced the same sensation again, as though someone was following her. She was no stranger to people keeping tabs on her. As a former Assistant District Attorney, many of her cases had involved unsavory characters and hardened thugs. Often, there were two sets of people that trailed her around the city, one bad, one good. Now in private practice, the list, more varied, included everything from murderers to white-collar criminals. The feeling grew stronger. She wasn't imagining it, but there were too many people around to prove her suspicions.

Waiting to cross the street, she read the huge sign describing the progress of the Southern Artery Project, known to the city as The Big Dig. Now as it was years behind schedule and several billion over budget, speculation as to when it would be finished was a constant topic of conversation. Lately, because the project was supported by federal funds, it was becoming a hot topic in Washington as well. Accusations of massive stealing and embezzlement had reached the national evening news.

She followed the crowd around the latest construction site and crossed under the Expressway, turning right to Hanover Street. The aroma of meatballs, cheese, garlic, tomato sauce and freshly baked bread and pastry greeted her as she entered the small intimate restaurant. Conlon was seated at a window table, complete with white linen and fresh flowers.

"I love a man who's always on time." She planted a kiss on his cheek and gratefully settled in a chair.

"That's easy. You're always ten minutes late,"

"I'm that predictable?"

"No," he smiled. "I know you try, but somehow you never quite manage. You should set your watch ten minutes ahead."

"At least, I'm always early for court."

The waiter served a dish of calamari, two plates, a bottle of wine and a basket of freshly baked bread, still warm from the oven.

"I gather we're having something special?"

"We're in luck. Angelo is cooking tonight. I told him to use his imagination." He scooped a portion of the appetizer on each of their plates and passed the breadbasket. "Tonight, no shop talk, unless of course, you have something to confess."

"How do you always know?"

"Your lower lip quivers ever so slightly when you're hiding something."

"Do I do that in court?"

"No, only when you're personally involved."

"I think I'm being followed. I felt it this afternoon and then again as I walked through Faneuil Hall."

"Did you spot anyone?"

"It was too crowded. Maybe it's just my imagination."

"Trust your instincts and keep your eyes open."

"There's something else. This morning someone tried to push Gamble in front of the train at Copley."

"Was he hurt?"

"No, but now he's sure he's on to something. I had lunch with him and one of his old colleagues."

"You mean one of his spy buddies. I don't like this."

"I suppose you could call him that. His name is Marko Bertoni."

"I know that name. He's famous for his underground activities during the war. He and Gamble were quite a pair."

"How is it you know so much about all this?"

"I've read quite a bit about the history of the CIA, especially its beginnings. Gamble, Marko and your father are mentioned quite often."

"I had no idea. Dad doesn't talk much about that period of his life. Marko seems like such a gentleman. Gamble asked him to do a little checking in Paris. He feels the whole network may be based there."

"A fair assumption. Actually, it's a good idea."

"It is. I thought you'd be furious."

"They're not amateurs. I'm sure they'll be careful. I'd never tell them that, of course, and don't you either."

"My lips are sealed, except when it comes to food. What have you found out?"

The waiter arrived with their salads and refilled the breadbasket.

"Not much. Interpol has very little for us. Their art experts do agree there may be something to Gamble's suspicions. Two agents are due here on a drug investigation in a few days and asked to interview Gamble."

"I'll tell him. He'll be glad to help. This case is bound to have lots of angles. It should be right up his alley."

"I have a feeling we're in for an interesting ride."

Chapter Four

It was nine in the morning when Gamble met Marko Bertoni at the outdoor cafe located a few doors away from the gallery. They ordered coffee and chose a sidewalk table where they could enjoy the morning sun and still have a clear view of the gallery entrance.

Gamble cast his gaze down the street. "Here comes our young sales associate. Very sweet, knows a little about art, but nothing about painting."

"She's quite lovely," noted Marko, sighing loudly. "If only I were a few years younger."

"A few? Besides, she's not your type, too superficial." He turned his attention back to the view. "We'll wait a few more minutes. Hopefully, DeLacroix will make his appearance."

"What exactly do you have in mind?"

"We need to light a fire under our opponents. Maybe if we arouse a little fear in the man, he'll lead us to whoever is in charge of this operation." He paused for a moment to think.

"How involved do you think the Major is?"

"Up to his ears, but he isn't capable of doing this alone. I'd stake my life on that."

Marko frowned. "And that is precisely what you may be doing. We've got to find out if Keegan is alive. I remember meeting some of his relatives during the war. Maybe one of them put this together. He could be the link."

"Here comes our little pigeon now. He's getting out of that black sedan that just pulled up in front of the building."

"Are you sure?"

"Our charming young clerk described him on my initial visit to his establishment and this one was at the gallery the other night. We'll give him a few minutes and then pay him a visit."

"You still haven't answered my question."

"I don't have a firm plan. Just follow my lead and use your imagination. Pretend it's 1960. I want to make him nervous."

Ten minutes later, the two men entered the gallery and began to look around. With a practiced eye, each looked the room over, checking for cameras, alarms and sensors as they strolled around the room pretending to examine the exhibit. A few minutes passed before the young lady joined them on the floor.

"How nice to see you again. And you've brought a friend. I hope you'll do more than window shop today."

"Actually, I'm here to see if you have any information on the paintings we discussed on my last visit. I'm sorry, I don't recall your name."

"It's Elena, Elena Lassiter. I don't have anything

new to tell you, but Mr. DeLacroix, the gallery owner is here this morning. Why don't we see if he can help you."

The two men followed her back to the office. DeLacroix, standing by the window in a poised stance, obviously expected them. Under scrutiny, he looked even worse than Gamble remembered. He wasn't pudgy; he was fat and not particularly fastidious about his appearance.

"Gentlemen, please come in. Elena told me of your interest in the paintings featured in our window last week."

"My name is Gamble Coulhoon and this is my partner, Marko Bertoni. We're collectors of a sort. The paintings interest us. They look familiar." Gamble could see the man's whole body stiffen. He was definitely frightened.

As Coulhoon continued the conversation, Bertoni casually found a seat and mentally inventoried the office, taking note of every detail.

"I'm sorry, but they're no longer available."

"Have they been sold?"

"I'm afraid so." DeLacroix searched for his handkerchief and wiped the sweat dripping from his forehead. His hand was shaking.

"Is there any way you could contact the new owners? I would like to meet them, and perhaps, for a reasonable price, persuade them to sell."

"I'm afraid that's not possible."

"Would you at least get in touch with them and ask?"

"I'll see what I can do, but please don't get your hopes up."

"That's all I can ask." Gamble extended his hand. "Thank you for your time."

"My pleasure, gentlemen. I hope I can be of service."

The two men left the gallery and made a casual retreat down the street. They were sure at least one pair of eyes followed their departure.

"He's frightened," said Marko. "Not used to this cloak and dagger business. A bit affected, I might add."

"He may be our weak link, my friend. What else did you see?"

"The place has a state-of-the-art alarm system, a little too elaborate, if you ask me. Art galleries need security, but this one tells me they've got a lot more than a few pieces of so-called modern art to protect."

"Any suggestions?"

"Part of the cache you're looking for. Drugs. Stolen jewelry. Guns. Who knows what."

"Then we're just going to have to find out."

"I don't like the sound of that."

"Yes, you do. You already confessed to boredom. Marko, my friend, we're going back into action."

With a new spring in their step, the two men walked back to the cafe, ordered and took the same seats they occupied previously.

"When he comes out, we're going to follow him," announced Gamble.

"In what? We seemed to have forgotten transportation."

"I doubt we'll need it. Look, here he comes now."

DeLacroix came out of the gallery and started walking in the opposite direction, oblivious to the two shadows, now attached to him at a discreet distance.

"He doesn't have a clue," said Marko. "Look at him racing down the sidewalk. He hasn't looked back once or stopped to look in the window. The whole Russian Army could be tailing him."

"I told you, the man is ill-prepared for a life of crime. First, we put a few things together, then we confront him. With any luck, he'll sing like a bird."

"You sound like an old film noir movie."

"You've been watching too much television."

They slowed to a walk as DeLacroix pressed the buzzer and entered a brownstone several blocks from the gallery. Marko ducked into a doorway to hide while Gamble checked the mailboxes. He came back in a couple of minutes.

"There's only one name, The Rhinehart Corporation, but two buzzers. Someone connected to the company must have an apartment on the top floor."

"The Major?"

"Maybe, or someone of more importance." Stepping from the shadows, he reached for his cell phone and dialed Jennifer's private number. She answered on the second ring.

"Jennifer, I need Brian's services."

"Where have you been? I've been trying to contact you all morning. Your cell phone was off and don't tell me it was an accident."

"Guilty as charged. Marko and I paid a visit to the gallery."

"You what?"

"I'll explain later. We followed DeLacroix to a brownstone on Essex. He's inside now."

"I'll have him there as soon as I can. And you two keep out of sight."

Gamble turned off the phone, put it back in his pocket, and slipped back into the doorway with his friend. Ten minutes later, a white van pulled up to the curb. It was Brian. The two men opened the back and climbed inside.

"Our friend DeLacroix is inside. He's very nervous." Gamble relaxed in one of the three empty captain's chairs.

"Who's he with?" asked Brian as he shut off the motor.

"Don't know. Do you have a camera?"

Brian pointed to the front passenger seat. "Loaded and ready to go. Even have a telephoto lens. Who else am I looking for?"

"Take a picture of anyone entering or leaving."

"Then you don't want the Frenchman tailed?"

"We'll follow him when he comes out, but I think he'll head back to the gallery."

Brian settled back, expecting a long wait. "All the comforts of home, gentlemen. Coffee? Even have TV."

"Thanks for the offer, but no." Gamble looked around the van. "Surveillance certainly has come a long way. Not like the old days, sitting in cold cars, standing in freezing rain, chasing the bad guys down dark alleys."

"Only the best. Jennifer believes in high tech and likes to keep her drones happy." He reached for the phone attached to the hump between the two front seats. "I'm supposed to check in once I've made contact. She worries about you."

"Make the call. She thinks I'm becoming a doddering old fool. I may be old. But the rest of it certainly does not describe me or Marko, for that matter."

Ten minutes later, DeLacroix appeared at the door alone. The two men waited until he passed the van, then climbed out, leaving Brian to play photographer. As they suspected, he headed back to the gallery. A few minutes later, they reentered the building. Elena Lassiter intercepted them as they started down the hall.

"He's expecting us." Gamble lied and proceeded to open the office door. They found the startled De-

Lacroix at his desk, visibly shaken, his face ashen.
Marko ushered the young girl from the room and shut
the door behind her.

"You two, back again?" DeLacroix tried unsuccess-
fully to control his voice, his affected manner and
composure a memory. "Don't come near me or I'll
call the police."

"What's the problem? You seem upset," said Gamble.

"I'm sorry, I can't help you. Please leave."

"I don't understand. I was hoping you could help
me with another problem."

"You don't fool me. I told you, I cannot help! Perhaps another galley, I'll be happy to recommend one."

"I don't understand your attitude, but I never force
my business upon anyone." Gamble placed his business card on the desk. "If you change your mind, you
can find me at this number."

DeLacroix opened the office door to find Elena Lassiter standing in the hall. "Please see that these gentlemen leave the building and call the police if they
come in here again."

"He's a bit agitated," offered Marko. "Give him a
few minutes." This time, they knew more than one
pair of eyes were watching as they left the building
and proceeded down the sidewalk.

"He's afraid," said Marko. "Something happened at
Rhinehart Corporation."

"You are the master of the understatement."

Sean Keegan watched from the shadow of the doorway across the street from the gallery. He waited until
Coulhoon and his companion left the scene before he
entered his car and drove away. DeLacroix was becoming a problem.

*   *   *

A few minutes later, Brian watched Major Stone leave the brownstone and head down the street away from him. He took several pictures from inside the van, then fell in behind the subject, staying several yards behind. Still holding the camera, he sauntered along trying to look like a tourist.

The Major turned left on Clarendon Street and crossed Boylston to the main branch of the public library. Using the side entrance, he entered the building and took the stairs to the second floor. Brian followed at a safe distance.

He watched as Stone met two men at the end of one of the stacks. He was too far away to hear the conversation, but recognized them, the O'Brian boys, two of Timmy Harrington's thugs. Their boss, one of Boston's most powerful crime lords, had his fingers in everything from the numbers racket to gun running for the homeland. Maybe Gamble was right. Someone else was pulling the strings.

He slipped down the next stack, quietly making his way to the end. By the time he was within earshot, the three had disbanded. Only the Major remained. A few minutes later, he left the building. Brian followed him back to the brownstone and continued his vigil.

Jennifer spent the morning in court. The under-age children of two major clients had been arrested while frequenting one of the many illegal clubs that constantly moved from address to address, skillfully avoiding the police. Court appearances of this nature were not usually within her scope of duties, but she agreed to represent at the request of the partners. She left the courthouse and walked to the Common. As she headed toward Charles Street, a tall elderly man dressed in tan corduroys and a tweed jacket with patches on the elbows, joined her. She gave him a closer look and recognized him immediately.

"You're Major Stone."

"Correct the first time, young lady. I was told you have a good head on your shoulders."

"I've been looking everywhere for you, along with every other investigative organization known to man."

"So I've been led to understand." He took her arm and steered her toward the row of green benches that lined the walkway. "I'd like a few moments of your time, if I may."

"Why not, I don't have anything to lose." They found an empty one under a tree and sat. "I'm waiting."

"You must know a great deal about me by now."

"Not enough. I do know that you are a very clever man, shrewd and quite capable of taking care of yourself. Other than that, I'm completely in the dark."

"I find that hard to believe. However, I'm not here to discuss my finer qualities." He reached into a brown paper bag and produced several peanuts still in their shells. He cracked a few open and threw the insides to a small group of pigeons waiting for their lunch. "They depend on humans to feed them, you see. They've become lazy. Symbiosis. Many people exhibit the same inadequateness. They're unable to survive on their own."

"Please get to the point, Major Stone."

"Forgive me. The elderly sometimes tend to ramble on. Your recent efforts regarding the two paintings that unfortunately found their way into the Bryson Gallery window are causing me a great deal of distress. If it were up to me, I would move my little operation away from your prying eyes."

"In other words, you'd disappear again."

"Exactly, but now I have associates who are firmly

entrenched in Boston and would take a dim view of me relocating at the present time. They are not very nice people, young lady. Violence is part of their repertoire and I would hate to see them practice it on you."

"Are you threatening me?"

"No. Gamble will tell you, I'm not a violent man. It's merely a friendly warning. Believe me, I would never do anything to harm you or our friend Gamble, for that matter. But I can't control the others." He threw the rest of the peanuts to his worshippers and stood up to leave. "Leave things alone. Stick to defending those who can afford your fees."

"Are you having me followed?"

"Again, no, but I'm sure you've made plenty of enemies in your line of work."

She remained on the bench and watched him walk away. The thought of following him surfaced for a moment, but she discarded it. A man who successfully evaded every major law enforcement agency in the world for more than fifty years would give her the slip in five minutes. She reflected on what had just transpired. Gamble and Marko were right. Stone may have pulled off a successful robbery, but murder was not part of his repertoire. She waited until he was out of sight, then walked slowly to her office. The meeting left her unsettled and full of questions.

Chapter Five

It was five A.M. when Conlon arrived at the crime scene. Another homicide. He wondered why murder victims always seemed to be discovered in the wee hours of the morning. A light drizzle, still lingering from a late evening storm, brushed against his face as he walked into the alley, carefully stepping around a deep puddle caused by runoff from the gutter. Hastily rigged spotlights spewed artificial light, casting an odd blue-white sheen on the landscape. The usual noise and controlled confusion swirled around the area as the technicians from the medical examiner's office plied their expertise. A sketch artist and cameraman judiciously captured every nuance for posterity.

"What have we got?" he asked one of the detectives.

"One of the neighborhood homeless found him in the trash. Seems the body was occupying his bed."

"Do we have an ID?"

"I fished his wallet out of his back pocket. André DeLacroix. Owns the gallery out front," said Atkins.

"That does it."

"You say something, Lieutenant?"

"No, nothing important. I don't suppose we got lucky and have two eyewitnesses that can identify the perp."

"Not yet."

Conlon walked closer to the body as two technicians pulled the corpse from the container and stretched the victim out on the pavement.

"Two taps to the head," said one. "Very neat. Must have been real close. Weapon of choice looks like a twenty-two. The slugs are still inside. They must have done a lot of damage. I'll know more once we do a work-up."

"See if you can hustle this one along." He turned to Klein and Atkins, the two detectives who answered the call. He considered them the best in the unit. "Canvas the neighborhood. You know the drill. Find out if anybody saw anything." As he looked around, he saw several sets of muddy footprints, some leading to the back door of the building. "What about the gallery?"

"Saully took videos, but be careful what you touch, the lab crew isn't finished yet."

He entered the building and followed the hallway to the office. As he stepped inside, he nodded to the woman busy dusting for prints. Nothing seemed out of order, nice and neat. No overturned lamps or broken furniture, no papers strewn on the floor, no opened drawers. A pool of blood, still damp, cast a large stain on the Oriental rug in front of the desk. The furnishings were mahogany; the chairs, upholstered in navy blue leather, and what looked like a state-of-the-art computer sat on a credenza against the back wall. Four posters of classic movies hung above it. Conlon assumed they were rare.

To his right stood a built-in bar, but no liquor, only bottled water. At least that was all he could see. Several paintings hung on the wall. Conlon couldn't tell what they were supposed to represent, but they certainly got his attention. Everything was understated, but expensive. The man certainly liked his creature comforts.

Pulling on latex gloves, he flipped through the victim's appointment book. It was filled with the names of art dealers and customers, all neatly identified. He found the sales assistant Elena Lassiter's phone number listed in the back on a separate page. After jotting down the information in his notebook, he left the building, explained to his detectives where he was going, and walked to his car.

As he pulled away, Conlon reached for his phone and dialed. Jennifer picked up on the third ring.

"Are you awake?"

"I am now. Conlon, it's Saturday morning. You know, the day I sleep in. I take that back. It's not even morning yet."

"I wouldn't be calling if it wasn't important."

"I know. Sorry to snap your head off, but you interrupted a dream. I was basking in the sun at a beautiful Caribbean resort, enjoying the full attention of several handsome men. They all looked like you."

"DeLacroix is dead. A homeless guy found him face-down in the trash in the alley behind the gallery."

"Great. Our only lead. Any clues?"

"No. I'm on my way to tell the assistant. I'll call you when I've got more. Go back to sleep."

To kill some time, he found an all-night coffee shop and ordered breakfast. A little after eight, he pulled up in front of the Lassiter girl's building and flipped his police business card on the dash. He was surprised to see that she lived in a waterfront condo near the Aquarium, one of the most expensive pieces of real estate in the city. He rang the bell and waited for a response through the intercom.

"Miss Lassiter, I'm Lieutenant Conlon with Homicide. Could I have a word with you?" He waited for the familiar click as the buzzer unlocked the outer door. Inside, he found the elevator and pressed the button marked four. She was waiting in the hall when he emerged.

"What's this all about?" she asked as she examined his credentials.

"Could we go inside?" He motioned toward the opened door to her apartment and followed her retreating form. His anticipation of luxury was not disappointed. Whoever was paying the tab had expensive taste. Thick carpets, wooden blinds, chrome furniture. He knew very little about decorating, but he knew this was way beyond his grasp. "I have some bad news. Mr. DeLacroix was found dead this morning at the gallery."

"What . . . what happened?" She gasped and steadied herself with back of the couch.

"Here." He offered his hand. "Someone shot him."

"Dear heaven, why?"

"I was hoping you could help me in that department. Your name was found in the back of his appointment book. I believe you are an employee."

"I don't know much about his private life. I've been working at the gallery for about seven months, but we didn't socialize. Where did you say they found him?"

"At the gallery. Did he have any problems with customers or artists, bill collectors, anyone?"

"There was one man, a Mr. Coulhoon and another man. I don't think he really knew them. They came by the gallery and asked about two paintings displayed in the gallery window last week. They had an argument and Mr. DeLacroix told me to call the police if they ever came back."

"What was the argument about?"

"I have no idea. I assumed it had to do with the paintings. The men left and I forgot about it."

"You'll have to come by the gallery and tell us if anything is missing. Do you feel up to it?"

"I'll be there later this morning, if that's all right."

Conlon nodded. "Thank you and I'm very sorry." He turned to leave. "I'll let myself out."

As he pulled into traffic, he reached for his phone. Jennifer, obviously awake by now, answered almost immediately.

"I've got bad news."

"How much worse can it get?"

"The gallery assistant said she heard Gamble trying to intimidate the victim yesterday. DeLacroix threatened to call the police."

"Have you told him about this?"

"Not yet, but he's got to come downtown."

"Give me a couple of hours. I'll have him in your office by eleven."

"See you then."

Jennifer hung up the phone and went to make some coffee. While waiting for it to brew, she dialed Gamble's number. "We have a problem," she said when he answered. "Our gallery owner is dead."

"When?" The voice was calm.

"Sometime last night. The police found him this morning. Did you threaten him?"

"Not exactly."

"His assistant tells a different story. They want to

talk to you downtown this morning. I told Conlon we'd be there by eleven."

"We? You think I need a lawyer?"

"Better safe than sorry, as they say. I'll be at your place by ten. Make sure you have a good story and order a cab. I don't want to spend an hour trying to find a parking space."

Next, she contacted Brian. "DeLacroix managed to get himself murdered last night."

"That certainly makes life a little more interesting."

"Conlon wants to see Gamble. It seems he threatened the victim yesterday in front of a witness. I'm going downtown with him."

"What do you want me to do?"

"He was killed at the gallery. See what you can find out. I don't think the police have had time to come up with anyone who'll admit they saw what happened. Check the neighbors. They might talk to you. I'll leave my cell phone on. Call me if you learn anything at all."

"I'll call in a few favors and get the scoop on the preliminary report. Talk to you later."

Chapter Six

Shortly after eleven, Jennifer and Gamble knocked on Conlon's office door. Jennifer shook her head at the mess. Papers were everywhere. They waited while he cleared off two chairs piled high with folders.

"Some of us don't have an army of secretaries and assistants," he said curtly. They settled in their seats while he searched for the needed information. "Why don't you tell me what went on yesterday and don't sanitize it. I want to hear it all."

Gamble gave him a brief overview of the conversation, leaving out very little. "I wanted to stir things up. It must have worked."

"It worked so well Interpol wants to talk to you. This murder has put a new twist on the subject."

"A new twist?"

"Why don't I let them tell you."

"I don't like the sound of this," said Jennifer as he left the room. "My instincts tell me this is not good."

Conlon returned with two men and made the introductions. Jennifer recognized both of them from a previous case. It had not been a happy association. The younger one, Benoit, was French, about forty, short and balding with the beginnings of a paunch. He was arrogant and didn't bother to hide his dislike for women who wanted to be in charge, especially intelligent and attractive ones.

Jennifer knew her premonition had been right. "This is not going to be easy," she whispered. "Follow my lead."

The older one, Langdon, was obviously in charge. He was a lean, compact, by-the-book looking man. He reminded Jennifer of Steve McQueen with his tight, precise movements. His accent, softened by years of travel, still held a hint of cockney. Selecting a chair, he pulled it away from the table and leaned it against the wall. He took a seat and waited for Gamble to open the discussion while his partner remained standing near the door. Nothing happened. His adversary had learned long ago that the one who spoke first was usually the loser.

Jennifer watched a smile spread across Conlon's face. She knew how much he enjoyed the whole scene. He loved to see a pro at work and Gamble was certainly one of the best.

The Interpol agent finally gave up. "Mr. Coulhoon," he said, glancing in Jennifer's direction. "We need to ask you a few questions, privately."

"I stay. Mr. Coulhoon is my client."

"You're his attorney, I gather. Do you feel your client needs one?"

"Let's not deal with semantics. I'm here to ensure that Mr. Coulhoon's answers are duly noted in the correct context."

Langdon frowned. "We might as well begin, Mr. Coulhoon."

"Ask away," replied Gamble. "Always happy to assist the authorities."

"What was your relationship to the deceased, André DeLacroix?"

"None."

"None. Are you saying, you didn't know this man?"

"I met him twice at his art gallery where I discovered the two stolen paintings displayed in the window."

"What did you talk about?"

"The paintings were gone. He told me they had been sold. I prodded him a bit, but he stuck to his story. I knew he was lying, of course, but couldn't prove it. I thanked him and left."

"And that was the last time you saw him?"

"A short time later, I, I mean we, my associate Marko Bertoni and I followed him to The Rhinehart Corporation in a brownstone on Essex, then back to the gallery. Something must have happened during the visit because he was quite agitated and ordered us to leave. What's this all about?"

The younger agent ignored the question. "That's a little farfetched, considering your past affiliation with the paintings." He left his position by the door and leaned into Gamble. Their faces were barely three inches apart. "I think you stumbled upon their little scheme and decided to cut yourself in. Only they said no. Maybe you worked out an arrangement with this Major, if there is such a person, and somehow convinced him to get rid of DeLacroix and put you in his place. I think you killed him."

"That's preposterous. Whatever for?"

"The money, of course. You're not immune to cash, are you?"

"Let's try and keep things on track," interrupted Conlon. "If it wasn't for Mr. Coulhoon, you wouldn't have a clue about any of this."

"And now, you're trying to implicate him," said Jennifer. "I think we're done here. Come on, Gamble, this interview is over."

"I'll be happy to aid you in your investigation, but I assure you, I am not involved." Gamble followed Jennifer as she reached the door.

Benoit gave them both a disgusted look. "Don't leave town, Coulhoon. I'm sure we'll have more questions."

"Mr. Coulhoon came here on his own accord. To reward him, you tried to put him through the wringer. From now on, he'll answer any appropriate questions after they've cleared through me."

Jennifer and Gamble left the station and hailed a cab. "They think I'm part of this whole scheme. Sometimes, it doesn't pay to be a law-abiding citizen."

"I wasn't much help. Benoit and I had a difference of opinion a couple of years ago when I was with the DA. He left empty-handed and was not happy. He'd love to take me down. Also, they can't get their hands on Stone, so you'll do. When they run a thorough check on you, they'll move on. On the other hand, your past might make them perk up their ears. You've got all the makings of a dynamite bad guy."

"That's a comforting thought."

"Don't worry, Conlon will clear things up. And there's always Dad. A word from him will take care of everything."

"You father's been out of the loop for a very long time."

"Doesn't matter. You know that."

"Let's change the subject. On a lighter note, when

are you and Conlon going to, as they say, tie the knot?"

"We've talked about it, but we're in no rush."

"Is that a nice way of saying mind your own business?"

"No, it means we've got more pressing matters to think about." She gave him an affectionate kiss on the cheek. "Don't worry, you'll be one of the first to know. I'm going to need someone to walk me down the aisle and I'm not sure Dad will be up to it."

"If I know Brand, he'll find the strength."

"By the way, what about Keegan? Is he still alive?"

"Marko asked me that. Obviously, I'll look into it."

When they reached Gamble's brownstone, Jennifer waited until he was safely inside and then directed the cabby to take her to the office. A whole day's work awaited. She was pleased to find several others, mostly young associates and a few secretaries, busy at work on a Saturday. She hated working in an empty office. Deserted buildings made her nervous.

Around seven, she walked the few blocks to a small quiet restaurant to meet Conlon. The hostess led them to a table away from the bar where they could enjoy some quiet conversation.

"How could those idiots think Gamble could possibly be involved in such a scheme?"

"In their defense, they don't know the man. They're between a rock and a hard place. If all this becomes public knowledge, the heat from the top will be unbearable. Cracking a case with these ramifications could be a real feather in someone's cap. Politics exists everywhere, especially in Interpol. They've got to come up with someone and Gamble is a perfect target. He's not exactly the guy next door."

"You're right, as usual. One more thing," she added. "Brian followed the Major from a brownstone on

Essex Street to the main library. He met two men in one of the stacks on the second floor. They were Timmy Harrington's men."

"You know where this mythical Major is and you didn't tell me. You're doing it to me again."

"I'm telling you now."

"Now is a little late, but let's not argue over it. Did Brian happen to hear what was said?"

"He was too far away. The name on the door of the brownstone says The Rhinehart Corporation, but there are two mailboxes and buzzers. Someone else occupies space in the building. I think the Major has an apartment there."

"Could be. I'll do some checking. It's probably leased or owned by a blind trust, but you never know."

The waiter finally arrived to take their order. Jennifer ordered steamers and a salad; Conlon chose roast beef. It would be a while before their meals would be served, but they weren't in any hurry.

"No more shop talk," Conlon proposed. "In fact, I think we should discuss spending a weekend at your place at the beach. We'll take Gamble and your dad. It would be great for everyone."

"Sounds like a plan."

"There is one more thing. The Major stopped me on the Common today."

"He did what? Someday, you're going to go too far. What is the matter with you?"

"He just wanted to talk." She could tell he was furious. "Don't get excited. He told me he abhorred violence." She waited for a reaction, but nothing happened, so she continued. "He said that he had some new business partners who weren't very nice and no, he didn't name them."

"He didn't need to. I'm sure it's Timmy Harrington and his associates. Otherwise, why would Stone meet two of his men? If there's a way to make money the wrong way, he's involved. How I'd like to nail him. His fingers are in every illegal activity in the city."

"Calm down, I wasn't in any danger."

"Maybe not from him, but Harrington, he's another story."

"He wouldn't go after me. I'm too well known."

"He may have his head on straight, but some of his boys forgot to line up when they were giving out brains. I don't like this one bit."

"I'll keep Brian with me for a while."

Two hours later, Conlon deposited Jennifer at her back door. Unfortunately, he was due back at the station. The flu-ravaged department demanded his attention. "Do something for me," he said as she put the key in the lock.

"Anything, you know that." She turned in response. "You've got that look in your eye. Don't tell me, you want me to drag out my gun."

"Sometimes, it's a necessity. I'm not an advocate for civilians carrying guns, but in this case . . ."

"I hate resorting to arming myself."

"Keep it with you, please."

"I'm way ahead of you. I cleaned and oiled it yesterday. It's by my bed."

"That's a start, but it won't do you any good stashed in a drawer. Tomorrow, it's in your bag or at least in your briefcase."

"I can just see me trying to get through the sensors at the courthouse." She laughed to lighten things up. She could tell by the look on his face that it wasn't working. "You win, I promise." She kissed him goodnight, wishing their schedules weren't so hectic. She watched him walk down the stairs and waited for the familiar click as the outer door locked automatically.

Once inside, she heated some hot chocolate and trudged to the third floor and bed.

Listening to the late news, she drank the rest of the cocoa and was about to plump the pillows when she heard the sound of metal scratching against metal. Pausing, she waited. She heard it again; this time there was a click. Someone was trying to pick the locks on her back door. The well-known feeling of excitement laced with fear gripped her body.

She reached for the phone and dialed 9-1-1. "This is Jennifer McCallum at two-one-one Beacon Street. Someone's trying to break in. I can hear them in the back hall."

"Please stay on the line, I'm alerting the patrol right now."

"Tell them to use the alley. The stairs to my apartment are in the back. I live on the top floors." Opening the drawer to the night table, she reached for the Lady Smith, a compact but powerful and accurate handgun, and along with the phone still in her hand, stepped into the hall, pausing at the top of the stairs. She was a good shot, not an expert, but capable of hitting a target, especially at close range.

Her father had introduced her to hand guns and the practice range when she was a teen-ager. A necessity, he said, it had to do with his job. The explanation had not been extensive, but was enough for Jennifer to take it seriously. She always carried it with her during her stint in the DA's office. Now, she kept it in a drawer, cleaned and oiled, hoping she would never actually have to pull the trigger.

Dear heaven. Please get here on time. "They're having trouble with the locks. I've got three. All new. They're supposed to be foolproof," she whispered.

"The patrol is on its way."

"I hope so because I really don't like this."

From the opened window, she heard the sound of a car stop in the alley. She hurried back to the bedroom as a second patrol car approached. Four uniformed policemen stepped from their cars. "They're still there," she whispered down to them.

One officer tried the door. It was open. "Stay out of the way," one called up to her. All four pulled their guns as the first uniform stepped inside.

"Don't worry. It's not my day to be a hero." She ran back to the landing and heard shouting, footfalls, and then a crash. All she could envision was a fight and someone tumbling down the stairs. Suddenly, there was a shout, some more shouting, a scuffle and then nothing. Every beat of her heart sounded like an explosion in the silence. Until the knock on the door.

She ran down the stairs, but stopped before opening the door. "It's all right, ma'am."

She looked through the peephole and saw a uniform standing in the hall. "Thank heaven," she whispered and opened the door, gun in hand. Recognizing one of the officers, she opened the door wider and lowered it to her side.

"Caught them in the act, at least one of them. We've got him downstairs. You want to see if you recognize him?"

She followed the officer down to the alley to find the one suspect up against the wall, hands behind his head, legs spread.

"We found these," said one uniform. He held up two guns and a computerized lock pick. "At least they're up to date."

"I'm sure you have permits for these weapons," said the other officer. "You recognize him?" she asked Jennifer.

"No, sorry."

"Well, I do," she replied. "Get him out of here."

She turned back to Jennifer. "If you'd come down to the station tomorrow and sign the complaint, we can wrap up the paperwork. Meanwhile, we'll let him enjoy the hospitality of the city for the night. Sorry, we couldn't catch the other one. He's probably disappeared into the woodwork by now."

Jennifer thanked the officers and turned to go back upstairs. Suddenly, a car pulled into the alley, hugging the wall as it screeched to a stop. Conlon stepped from the car and approached the group. He took one look at the thug and reached for Jennifer.

"I'm fine," she said, grateful to feel his arms around her. "Boston's finest arrived in the nick of time."

"Well, well, look who we have here, one of the O'Brian boys, Terrance, isn't it? He's one of Timmy Harrington's hatchet men. I'll have to take care of this personally. Take him down to the station. I'll be along in a few minutes."

He turned to Jennifer. "Let's get you upstairs." He opened the door and followed her inside. "I leave you alone for ten minutes and what do I find, you, four cops and some small-time thug having a party in the alley. Glad to see you're packing artillery," he whispered, glancing down at the gun as they climbed the stairs.

"You don't think this is a simple break-in, do you?" she asked, once they were inside the apartment.

"He's nickel-and-dime stuff, but his boss isn't. Besides, he doesn't deal in this kind of thing, unless someone put them up to it. He more into breaking legs and scaring defenseless deadbeat losers. I'll post someone in front of the building and have the patrol make a few extra sweeps through the alley, though I don't think you'll have any more trouble tonight."

"Gamble gave me a disk with all his notes and pictures, but no one knows about it. And why would one of Harrington's men be interested?"

"Maybe they think he gave you the original hand-written list or a copy of it. Will you be all right?"

"I'll be fine."

"Lock the door and try and relax. I've got to get back. Maybe Terrance can tell us what this is all about, but I doubt he'll talk. I'll call you after I talk to him."

He left Jennifer and rode back to the station where he found the O'Brian boy waiting for him in one of the interrogation rooms. He was the usual strong-arm type, long on brawn and short on brains. He joined two detectives in their questioning.

"You made a bad mistake tonight," he began. "Don't you know you never make trouble for friends and relatives of the cops? I know you're dumb, but I didn't think you were that stupid."

"I've got nothin' to say until my lawyer gets here," said Terrance.

"Two men have been following the lady. If I find out you two are involved, it's not going to be pleasant. Not only is she a friend of mine, but she's an officer of the court, and a former District Attorney."

"I've got nothin' to say."

"Has he been booked?"

"Yeah. Only took a couple of minutes. He's been arrested so many times, the computer had all the information. Look at his rap sheet. It's a mile long."

"See if you can lose him in the system. Maybe if he cools his heels with the druggies and the rest of the scum we deal with, they might be a bit more cooperative."

Chapter Seven

The next few days were quiet. The police and Interpol continued with their investigations. The leads went nowhere. The dead man's business ventures were tied up in dummy corporations and foreign partnerships. DeLacroix's accountant had almost no knowledge of the man's affairs. His only contact with the man had been preparing the corporate income tax returns. His private life remained a mystery and there was no sign of the Major.

Interpol began digging into international connections. They found a few. The parent company, Air International, was based in Paris. Tracing the owner, investigators found it was an old company, formed right after the war, still in existence, dealing in international shipping. Two men were assigned to investigate. Conlon tried to dissuade the two agents in Boston, but they continued to delve into Gamble's past. They still considered him their best suspect.

The gallery continued to operate. Silent partners, legitimate ones it appeared, planned the shows and continued buying and selling for their clients, but on a much smaller scale. The police could find no connection with an international stolen art ring.

Conlon called a meeting with Atkins and Klein. They were a good team. Atkins, a seasoned by-the-book investigator with nearly twenty years of experience and Klein, a young hotshot, a little impulsive, but careful and intuitive, up on all the latest technical gadgets now part of the job. The two refilled their coffee cups and joined him in his office.

"Tell me what you've got on the DeLacroix murder."

"First, no one saw anything. The shots were fired inside the gallery so that may be true." Klein whipped out his notebook and referred to his notes. "André DeLacroix, forty-four years old, a French citizen. Divorced, two children and an ex-wife living in Paris. Pays a hefty sum in alimony and child support. Works for Art International. He's a relative of some sort, but doesn't have ownership in the company. It's still a private corporation, owned by the same family since before the war. On the surface, he seems like a regular guy. The deceased was in charge of acquisitions, I think that's the word." Klein laughed. "I'm learning the lingo."

Conlon and Atkins rolled their eyes.

"Anyway, he buys the stuff for the business here in Boston, but there are a lot of imports and exports too."

"Those two words always spell trouble for me," said Atkins.

"DeLacroix made a lot of trips to Europe last year. Once a month or so he would go to Paris with little side trips to London and Zurich. Company credit cards show lots of charges, jewelry, expensive hotels, gadgets, and cell phone rentals. Rumor has it he had something going on the side with the lovely Elena Lassiter. There's a whole lot of charges to Esprit Florist for flowers delivered to her address."

"It must have slipped her mind," said Conlon dryly. "She told me she didn't know anything about his private life. What have you got on her?"

Atkins skipped over a few pages and continued. "Elena Lassiter, born Chicago, 1966. Education, University of Wisconsin at Madison; Human Resources.

"She worked at the Chicago Museum of Art for a couple of years and moved to Boston in February of '96. Had a couple of jobs and began working at the gallery in October of last year. She lives in a pretty expensive place down on the water."

"I was there. It's plush," said Conlon. "Find out who's paying the rent. Ten bucks says it was De-Lacroix."

"I checked Passport Control. She's been hopping around the continent too. Funny thing, her trips all happened about the same time as her boss."

"So she lied," said Klein. "Maybe she didn't want anyone to know she and the boss had a thing going."

"Or, she's got something to hide. I'll have to pay her another visit. Maybe at the gallery. Then I'll get Jennifer to get a handle on the lady's finances. She's got more resources for that kind of thing than we do. The lovely Elena better have another sugar daddy in the wings or she'll be joining the common folk."

"You want we should go?"

"No, the Chief wants action from me personally and you know what that means." Conlon stretched and leaned back in his chair. The old pre-war oak frame creaked under his weight. "Better I take the heat than you guys. Just keep plugging. Also, find out about this Rhinehart Corporation and see if there's anything on a Sean Keegan. Supposed to have disappeared in Paris right after the war."

"That should be easy."

"He lived here before he joined the Army. Maybe you can dig up something on the family. And see if there's any connection between the deceased and my favorite crook, Timmy Harrington."

Atkins let out a soft whistle. "We're talking bad guys here." He motioned to his partner. "Come on, pal, we've got work to do." The left Conlon to ponder his options.

He knew they were getting nowhere. The medical examiner's report hadn't produced any leads so he decided to make a trip to Albany Street and talk to the horse's mouth herself, Barbara Washington, chief medical examiner for the county. He stopped at a small Chinese market and bought a can of specially mixed tea, a small bribe, and two roast-beef sandwiches from the deli next to it. Conlon and the medical examiner were fast friends and often did off-the-record favors for each other.

A few minutes later he arrived at his destination. "Anyone in?" he called from the outer office.

"I'd know that voice anywhere. In back."

Conlon inched around several huge piles of files and found her in the tiny kitchen at the far end of the room. "Your office is worse than mine," he commented as her handed her their lunch. "Maybe that's why we get along."

She opened the bag and checked the label on the tin. "My penchant and lunch too. My, my. You must want something awfully bad."

He found an empty chair and slowly dropped into it. "It's the DeLacroix case. I'm getting nowhere. Any minute I expect to be called on the carpet. The beautiful people don't like having murder committed on their turf."

"Let me see what I can do for you. Open the sand-wiches while I look for your file."

"How can you find anything in this place?"

"Look who's calling the kettle black," she called from the outer office. "I've seen your filing system, remember? Besides, it's an art, one you may acquire in good time." She returned with a slim manila folder as Conlon placed the opened plastic wrapper on the desk. "Let's see." She began flipping through the pages.

"Our victim was killed with a twenty-two caliber. Two bullets in the back of the head. Very close range. The barrel must have been touching the back of his skull. Lots of powder burns. Up close and personal, to say the least. The bullets were still inside. They rattled inside and did a lot of damage. I've got them and they're in surprisingly good shape."

"Enough for a match? Not that we'll ever find the gun."

"We could make a pretty good ID. In court, it might be shaky."

"Time of death?"

"Sometime between one and three in the A.M."

"Anything else? No great clues?"

"The guy lived well, lots of alcohol, some drugs. Running to fat, but on the whole, not in bad shape. Clues, not really, but I'll give it another go. Things are a little slow and I have some free time."

They finished their lunch and enjoyed a few minutes of good conversation, both free from the rigors of their respective jobs. As he left the building, Conlon's beeper went off.

Ten minutes later, he was cooling his heels in the police chief's outer office at Schroader Plaza. He read a magazine until his boss's secretary opened the door and motioned him into the inner sanctum. The Chief was behind his desk, jacket off and cuffs rolled back, talking on the phone. Conlon took a seat and waited.

"Now," the Chief began as he hung up the receiver. "Where are we on this gallery thing? I'm getting all kinds of heat from the movers and shakers. They don't like violent crime on their turf."

"We don't have much, Sir. The man was killed inside his gallery and dragged out to the back alley by one or more persons. He may have been involved with an international ring dealing with stolen art, but that's only a theory at the moment."

"Is that why Interpol is concerned? I don't like them nosing around in our investigations."

"I'm doing my best to keep them out of it, Sir."

"And what about this Coulhoon character? I've been told he worked for Brand McCallum and the CIA at one time. What's he got to do with all this?"

"He's the one who discovered the stolen art ring. He's not really a player. I'm using him as a consultant. Interpol likes him for a suspect, but I doubt it. He's not capable."

"What do you mean, not capable! He was a hotshot CIA agent, a legendary black bag man."

"That was years ago. He's nearly eighty."

"So he forgets? I don't think so. Just because he's a pal of Brand McCallum and your girlfriend doesn't mean he gets special treatment."

"Yes sir, but—"

"Don't 'but' me. Do your job." The Chief took a deep breath. "Look, I don't think he did it. He's too smart to leave any evidence, especially a body. Make everyone happy. Make me happy. Make Interpol happy. Cooperate with them, but it's our case. I don't want the CIA, Interpol or anyone else picking our pocket on this one. Deal with it. The neighborhood alliance is all over the Department. The merchants and the residents are up in arms. And it's no good for the city or for tourism, for that matter. This is affecting everything from the Freedom Trail to the Swan Boats. Conventioneers are afraid to bring their families to the city and mothers don't want their kids in the Public Garden."

The Chief paused to clear his throat. "We need this thing gone."

Dismissed, Conlon went back to his office no worse for wear, having been through it all before. He plowed through the never-ending paper work that filled his "in" basket and left the office around seven to pick up Jennifer.

The temperature had dropped considerably as the sun dipped in the west. The warm spring day was now a cool crisp evening. Jennifer, dressed in jeans and a navy sweater, sat waiting for him on the front steps of her building. She climbed in the car and they headed for Beacon Hill to have dinner with Brand McCallum, Jennifer's father.

Conlon eluded the one-way streets and, using the back alleys, cut their driving time to a few short minutes. Parking was by permit only, but the McCallum residence was one of the few that had two empty off-street spaces. The two entered the rear entrance of the house and found the owner and his housekeeper on the small terrace overlooking a tiny English garden. Brand was tolerating a cocktail of iced tea while Maribel was busying arranging a table for dinner.

"Jennifer, Conlon," greeted her father. "You're right on time. Now that the cocktail hour is forbidden, I dine early. I hope you don't mind."

"Of course not, Dad." Jennifer gave him a kiss

while he and Conlon shook hands. She poured two glasses of tea and handed one to Conlon. "You two keep each other company while I help Maribel serve dinner up here."

"How's the case coming, young man?"

"Slowly, that's about all I can say. We're looking at several angles, but haven't made much progress." He spent the next few minutes filling him in on the story.

"I don't want to see Gamble's reputation smeared so that some bureaucrat can keep his ego intact. If you need any help from me, you just ask for it."

"Thanks, I'll remember that."

"When are you going to make an honest woman of my daughter?"

"Whenever she agrees. I guess she still needs more time. We've talked about it, but she's not quite ready to set the date. Next year, maybe."

"She's headstrong and independent, but anything you two decide, you have my blessing."

"I appreciate that."

"What are you two conspiring about?" Jennifer came through the door with a tray filled with place settings and condiments.

"Nothing, my dear," replied her father. "Just shop talk."

"I bet. Save it for dinner. I need to pick your brain."

Maribel appeared behind her carrying dinner on a large tray, and the women arranged the dishes on the sideboard. Jennifer prepared a plate for her father and Conlon helped himself. The housekeeper left them to their conversation for her seven o'clock quiz show.

"Dad, give us your opinion on this whole mess." She filled her plate and joined them at the table.

"I think Gamble has stumbled on an extremely efficient combination method of selling stolen art and transporting guns to Ireland. I also think you should concentrate on the art and let some other branch of the government deal with the guns."

"What if they're so intertwined, they can't be separated?" asked Conlon.

"Don't get involved with that end of it. You'll never win. Besides, I don't think Timmy Harrington has anything to do with the murder. He wouldn't want to jeopardize this new route. No, it strikes me as a crime of passion, not love or remorse, but one of desperation, related to the art aspect. Someone panicked and showed very poor judgment and that's not Tim Harrington's style."

Interpol requested a second meeting with Gamble. Jennifer went to the station with him. The same two investigators were there to greet them in one of the interrogation rooms. No informal meeting in a cozy office this time.

"Mr. Coulhoon, you seem to have a considerable number of friends in high places."

"I've been around a long time, even longer than you." Gamble chuckled at his own joke.

The agent didn't seem to enjoy the humor, ignoring the barb. "Everyone seems to vouch for your character. Some think you're the reincarnation of Sherlock Holmes."

"You're too kind," he replied wryly.

"Let's not play games. We have a job to do and it would be in your best interest to help and not get in the way."

"Inspector, you seem to have a problem with me. Why, I don't know, but I will tell you for the last time, I had no connection with this man. I saw the paintings and decided to follow up on them. That's all."

"Do we have new ground to cover?" asked Jennifer. "If not—"

"Actually we do. Mr. Coulhoon, do you have more than one bank account?"

"Yes. I have several, some here, others abroad. I also have a stock portfolio, some mutual funds and real estate holdings. What are you getting at?"

"Considering your pension and salary from the university, wouldn't you say that's a bit much?"

"Over the years, I invested my money wisely."

"You made a rather large deposit to one of your U.S. accounts in the amount of . . ." He picked up a piece of paper from the table. "In the amount of three hundred-seventy-two thousand dollars and change on April the twenty-sixth. Where did it come from?"

"Don't answer that," said Jennifer.

"Let's move on then. A few years before you left the government, there was an investigation concerning those investments."

"Yes, and if you bothered to look further, you would have seen that I was cleared of all charges."

"So it seems, but I believe where there's smoke, there's fire. Don't you agree?"

"On occasion, but this doesn't happen to be one of them."

The second agent took over the questioning. He wasn't as polite. "You never did give us an alibi."

"You never asked."

"Well, we're asking now, wise guy. Where were you on the night of the murder?"

"I went to the Museum of Art. There was an exhibit of Impressionists I wanted to see."

"Did anyone go with you?"

"No, I rather enjoy these occasions alone, no chit-chat, if you know what I mean."

"What time was that?"

"I arrived at the museum about six and left around eight."

"Then what?"

"I took the subway to Copley and walked home."

"Did you stop anywhere?"

"There's a small grocery near my apartment that has a hot and cold buffet to go. I assembled a meal and went home. I read for an hour and turned out the light about eleven. And no, there's no one to verify it, no visitors, no phone calls. I didn't know I would be needing an alibi."

"You seem to have the local police buffaloed. Your lawyer probably has something to do with it, but she doesn't carry any weight with us. We know you're up to your neck in this and we're going to prove it," Benoit sneered.

"Are we done here?" Jennifer was furious and did nothing to hide it.

"Don't leave town, Mr. Coulhoon."

"I'm at your disposal. Gentlemen, always a pleasure."

Conlon followed the two of them out in the corridor. "Sorry about that. I tried talking to them, but they're convinced you're involved."

"Thanks for your help. I guess we're going to have to do this ourselves. By the way, aren't those boys treading on your turf?"

"Sort of, but I've been told to play nice. Don't worry, they're not taking over. They just think they are."

"Come on Gamble, let's get out of here before they change their minds." Once outside, she put the same question to him. "Where did you get the money?"

"I transferred it from an offshore account. The Talbot auction is next week. You know I always attend."

Chapter Eight

The next morning, Jennifer joined her running group for their usual three-mile run followed by breakfast. Leaving the deli, she stopped two of them and asked them to meet at her house that evening.

Brian was waiting when she returned to her office. He looked tired and out of sorts.

"What's wrong? You look terrible."

"I spent last night touring the restaurants and bars in a four-block area of the gallery. I'm too old for this stuff. Anyway, DeLacroix is well known on the street, liked to eat well and mingle with the beautiful people. The help loved him. He was a heavy tipper."

"I'm sure they're going to miss their meal ticket."

"It seems DeLacroix spent the last evening of his life all bent out of shape. He had a few drinks at that French place across the street. He told Tony, the bartender that he was thinking of taking a long vacation and maybe relocating to San Francisco or London. He also said DeLacroix was very nervous and not himself."

"What time did he leave?"

"He hung around until midnight and then went back to the gallery. Tony saw him go in the front door. A few minutes later, two guys followed him inside."

"Did DeLacroix let them in?"

"That's the funny part. It looked like they had a key."

"Did this Tony get a look at them?"

"It was dark, but he thinks he could probably identify them if he saw them again. He said they stayed in there for a long time. Then as he was locking up, all the lights went off in the gallery, but no one came out. As he crossed the street, he heard some sounds coming from the alley, but didn't pay any attention to them. He thought it was that old guy who sleeps back there, in the Dumpster, but when he got to the corner, he noticed someone in the alley, walking away in the other direction. He didn't see the guy's face, but the back door to the gallery was open."

"Was it one of the men he saw before?"

"He's not sure."

"What did he look like?"

"Average, not too tall. He walked pretty fast, so he couldn't be too old."

"Have the police questioned this Tony?"

"Not yet, but they'll get to him. They probably don't think anyone was in the restaurant at that hour."

"Keep digging, we need more than that."

"Can do. I'll see you later."

She spent the afternoon preparing for court. Two cases were pending; court dates had not been set, but she needed to be ready. She assigned each one to a different associate to complete the research and present it at a meeting set for the following week. Neither one appeared to be difficult, but they both involved important clients. A dog-and-pony show was in order.

She left the building before five and arrived home in plenty of time to shower and change before Brian, Gamble, and her two guests arrived. They joined her on the terrace where she told them of her plan.

Donna Bourdeau was an architect for one of Boston's biggest firms. She had contacts everywhere and often used them for Jennifer. Bob Turner, a web site designer, had all the tools to find anything available on line. His expertise would be more than enough to cover that area. The plus was these two were active in local theater.

"I have something special for you, if you're up to it. It's not dangerous; in fact, it might be fun."

"Shoot, we're listening," said Donna.

"I want you two to pose as a couple of art collectors. You're married and have lots of cash. Go to the gallery. Modern art is not your fancy, but someone told you that two Impressionists paintings had been displayed in the window a few days ago. You want to see them with a possible purchase in mind." She showed the photographs of the pictures in question. "They'll tell you they've already been sold. See if they can get the paintings back for your inspection. One of you will be wired and Brian will be outside listening to every word. The first sign of trouble and he'll come to the rescue."

"That doesn't sound too difficult."

"The minute I hear anything unusual, I'll be there in a flash."

The two looked at each other and nodded their heads. "Count us in," said Bob. "When and where?"

"How about late Wednesday morning, about eleven. Come here first. Brian will wire you up and you can walk there from here. He'll be parked in his van a couple of doors down. Any questions?"

"No, sounds pretty straightforward."

Jennifer reached for some papers on the table. "I need a few more things. Check out these two companies, The Bryson Gallery and The Rhinehart Corporation. Find out everything: subsidiaries, officers, the works. Then, DeLacroix's finances. He's the art dealer that was killed a few days ago."

"Are you defending someone?"

"Not yet. We're trying a little preventive medicine. Delve into his tax returns, personal and corporate credit cards, any real estate, his ex-wife and children."

"I take it we're looking for something special."

"Unexplained money and his relationship to this Rhinehart Corporation. Also, who is this Elena Lassiter."

"It may take some time."

"We don't have it." She walked them to the door. "I appreciate your help. See you Wednesday."

"What would I do without them?" she asked Brian as she closed the door. "They are the best."

"Conlon's not going to like this."

"He won't know 'til it's over and then it will be too late. Besides, if we prove our point, what can he say?"

"Tell him when I'm not around. I don't want to see it."

"Do you think it will work?" she asked.

"Greed always wins out," replied Gamble, looking at his watch. "It's time this old man retired for the evening."

"I'll walk you home," said Brian.

"No, no, it's only a few blocks. Besides, you two have some planning to do."

She walked him to the door and returned to find

Brian at the window. "I don't like this. I'm going to follow him."

"He won't like it."

"He won't know. He's sharp, but I'm very good. If I must say so myself." He looked back out the window. "I can still see him, but in another minute or so, he'll be out of sight."

Suddenly a black car pulled up to the curb and two men got out. Brian bolted for the door. "We've got trouble. Call the police."

Jennifer watched the two men fall in behind Gamble. She reached for her mobile on the table and punched 911.

"This is Jennifer McCallum at two-one-one Beacon Street. There's a mugging taking place outside my window. Please hurry." She stayed on the line and ran down the stairs out to the sidewalk. She could see Brian following the two men down the sidewalk. Suddenly, he began running, shouting as he closed the gap.

The two men turned. Jennifer could see one pull a gun from his waist and aim. She ran into a doorway and watched as Brian ducked and fired three quick shots, wounding one. She could see Gamble in the distance running toward them.

The second man grabbed his accomplice by the arm and dashed across the street. He fired two shots in Brian's direction just before they disappeared into an alley. Gamble and Jennifer arrived at Brian's side as a police cruiser pulled around the corner, its siren piercing the air. It screeched to a stop and the two officers jumped out.

"They went into the alley," said Jennifer. "Two of them."

"Are you folks all right?" asked one. They all nodded and watched as the uniforms ran into the alley.

"They're long gone," said Brian.

The two officers were back in a matter of minutes. "You recognize them?"

"It was too dark, but their car is parked down the street, the black Caddie."

"Probably stolen, but we'll check it out. I'll file a report, but there's not much more we can do. I'd advise you get inside."

"Good advice," said Gamble. "Thanks for your help. Meanwhile, Jennifer, we'll get you safely upstairs and then I'll take Brian up on his offer."

On Wednesday morning, Brian took up his vigil several doors down from the gallery and settled in with his thermos of coffee and the morning *Globe*. A few minutes later, he spotted his colleagues strolling down the sidewalk right on time. As they entered the gallery, he set the paper aside and concentrated on the tiny listening device in his left ear. The reception was loud and clear.

The same young lady greeted them as they strolled around the room. "Good morning and welcome to our gallery. My name is Elena Lassiter. I don't seem to recognize you. Have you been here before?"

"No," said Bob. "We're the Henleys. This is my wife, Joan and I'm Richard. I understand this gallery usually deals with modern art, but we were told that you had two Impressionist paintings in your possession."

"We did, but I think they've been sold."

"So soon? Is there any way you could locate the new buyers and see if they would be willing to sell?"

"I'm not sure. Unfortunately, the gallery owner was killed in a senseless robbery a few days ago. Right now, we're a little disorganized, but if you'll leave your name and number, perhaps I can help you."

"We'll be out most of the day and we're leaving town on Friday. I'll give you my cell phone number. That way you can locate us no matter where we are."

"Sounds perfect. Meanwhile, I'll see what I can do."

"Oh," added Donna. "We believe these paintings may be part of a set of four. If reunited, they could be priceless."

Donna wrote down the number and the two left the gallery, retracing their steps. Brian drove his van in a nearby alley and picked them up.

"You were perfect. Couldn't have done better myself."

"Thanks. Now what?" asked Donna.

"We wait. Meanwhile, we can kill some time. I know a great place for pizza."

They didn't have long to wait. The phone rang at one o'clock. "Mr. Henley, I've located the owner of the paintings. He's agreed to consider selling."

"That's wonderful. When can we see them?"

"Give me a few days. I may be able to locate the other two paintings you mentioned. Why don't I call you when you get back from your weekend."

"Sounds perfect. I look forward to your call." A grin spread across his face as he disconnected the call. "I love doing stuff like this."

By Friday, Jennifer was ready for a little relaxation. She, Conlon, her father, Gamble, and Marko headed for Maine and the family cottage. They left early to avoid the weekend traffic and with Conlon driving her sport utility, stopped at the gate just before five. The guard passed them through and they arrived at the weather-beaten house facing the water a few minutes later.

The cottage was a large rambling wooden structure built around the turn of the century. It was one of eight homes that shared a private beach and a security guard. Unpretentious, it served as a getaway for members of the family; a place to enjoy nature and good company without the interruptions of the world.

All eight owners were original; all knew each other and respected each other's privacy. Twice a year, on the Fourth of July and Labor Day, the annual parties were held, complete with a clambake, sailing, and fireworks. Children made lifetime friends. It was a wonderful place, at least according to Jennifer.

Conlon and Jennifer unloaded the car and deposited the luggage on the second floor. Brand McCallum, with a little help from Gamble, settled in a wicker chair on the porch. Though the trip had not been a long one, he was drained.

Marko helped Jennifer put the groceries away and poured some iced tea into a pitcher. "The sea air will do your father good."

"He's so frail, Marko. I worry all the time."

"He's stubborn. He'll be around for a few more years."

"I hope so." She sliced some cheese and put it on a plate along with some crackers. "We'll put steaks on the grill tonight. How does that sound?"

"Perfect. Now, you go out, sit by your father, and soak up some of that sun. I'll put the rest of this away."

Jennifer took the tray to the porch, where she found her father and Gamble deep in conversation. "Is this a private discussion or can I join in?"

"Actually, it concerns you," said her father. "Gamble's been filling me in on his problem. Between the five of us, I'm sure we can find some answers."

"I hope you're right," said Conlon as he joined them. "I've tried to convince Interpol that they're barking up the wrong tree, but they're convinced Gamble's their man."

"That's because it's the easiest route. They don't have to think," said Jennifer. "I'm afraid they'll go to the police and convince them he's guilty."

"I've already voiced my opinion, but Jennifer's right, they may go over my head."

"Then we're going to have to beat them to the punch." Brand pointed to the pitcher. "The doctors have banished alcohol from my daily regime, so I guess it will have to be iced tea."

She filled the glasses and passed the cheese and crackers around. She then told them about Brian and his trip to the library.

"Timmy Harrington is a shrewd, dangerous man who runs his organization with an iron hand. He really believes he's a patriot striking a blow for freedom. That makes him even more dangerous. He's got his fingers in so many places, it's hard to guess which one to pursue," said Brand.

"I vote for two," said Conlon. "Narcotics or guns."

"What would art thieves know about either of them?" she asked.

"They don't need to have any expertise," injected her father. "Narcotics smugglers and gun runners have one thing in common with them; they need a way to get their product from one country to another without it being confiscated by customs officials.

"It would appear that this particular group has operated a very successful route for nearly fifty years. If it worked for them, it would certainly work for guns, drugs, money, jewels, anything illegal. Let's suppose Harrington approached the Major and suggested a partnership. The Major would share his system in return for a fee and protection. Each would retain control of his own operation with no interference from the other and their bank accounts would remain separate. Harrington would have a safe route for his product and the Major would increase his coffers and be assured his merchandise would be safe from theft. It's a perfect arrangement. Everybody wins."

"There's something else," said Jennifer.

"Don't tell me," said Conlon. "Your little friends. What are they up to?"

"Two of them, posing as art lovers, went to the gallery. They asked about the two paintings."

"Who did they talk to?"

"That young assistant. She says she contacted the new owners and they're willing to consider selling. Someone in the organization must have told her what to say. I don't think she's knows what's really going on. She's trying to set up a meeting."

"You think she's in on all this?" he asked.

"Donna mentioned the other two pictures."

"What other two pictures?" asked Conlon. "You've been holding out."

"There are four paintings in all. Two of them were part of the stolen collection, but there are two more, owned by a young lady here in Boston. They belonged to her parents in Germany. Before they were taken to the camps, they were able to smuggle some of their belongings out of the country along with the two children. An old friend kept them in London. The daughter married an American and lives here. I've consulted with her many times. She's a restorer working at the art museum."

"Does anyone else know about these paintings?"

"I suppose so, it's no secret, but then, it's hardly public either."

"Contact this woman and see if she's been approached. Let's see how much these people know," said Conlon.

"All this still doesn't answer the question, who killed DeLacroix? Was it Stone?"

"I'm not so sure about that," said Gamble. "He must have learned a few tricks over the years, but for cloak and dagger, I doubt it. He assumed I was a simple clerk who had some knowledge of art. I'm sure he never knew I was involved in more clandestine activities and I'll bet he doesn't suspect that I've tracked a lot of his sales over the years. Besides, he doesn't have the stomach to kill someone."

"Then who's behind it?" asked Conlon.

"I don't know, but if I don't find out, I may be spending the rest of my days in a six-by-nine cell with no amenities."

Elena Lassiter locked the front door of the gallery and shut off the lights in the main viewing area, leaving on a series of tiny spotlights to guide her retreat to the office. Everyone else was gone. Once inside, she shut off the surveillance cameras and went to work.

Hidden in a small box on top of the credenza behind the desk, she found the keys to the filing cabinet and unlocked the bottom drawer. She pulled a folder from the back and, using the machine near the window, began copying the contents. Ten minutes later, she left with her attaché stuffed with reading material.

She stopped for takeout at a Chinese place near her apartment and went home. As the food heated in the microwave, she undressed, washed the day's pollution from her face and hands, and returned to the kitchen for a quick meal, ready for the long night ahead.

This was not a whim, for she knew the consequences if she was caught. For several weeks, she had observed unusual things happening at the gallery. Small, seemingly inconsequential unrelated instances, but together, added up to something wrong. Ever since that Mr. Coulhoon's visit. Long involved meetings held after hours, lots of faxes, extra deliveries of things not ordered or entered in the inventory list. Files had disappeared and the new manager was always at the computer and on the phone.

One room in the storage area in back now had a padlock on it. René had the key for a while, but since his death, she didn't have any idea where it was. The once silent partners now seemed to be running the operation. They treated her more like a clerk instead of an experienced employee.

She wasn't even allowed to make the deposits to the bank anymore. She wanted the job back, for it gave her a half-hour to window shop the area stores. She missed her few minutes of harmless flirting with Tommy, who worked in the ice cream parlor and was nearly through the list of twenty flavors.

It would be easy to get another job, for René had introduced her to Boston's art scene. She was a quick study and any of the local galleries would be happy to hire her. Learning other aspects of the trade would not be difficult. But with René gone, her lifestyle was on the verge of an abrupt change. She needed cash or someone else to pick up the bills. The five-thousand-dollar-a-month rent was not in her budget, and she could wave goodbye to any expensive jaunts to Europe. Maybe Taylor, the new manager, might be interested in a little R and R.

Her new bosses frightened her. She wasn't sure they even knew anything about art, for they showed little interest in sales. The artists were not being promoted and sales were down. All their attention was on deliveries, checking to see if they were on time and the number of boxes that arrived.

Her suspicions were getting the best of her. Every

night for the last ten days, she stayed late and copied one file. So far, she found nothing suspicious, but she was determined to keep looking. She poured a glass of milk, and with pen in hand began scanning the pages as she ate. When she finished, she set everything aside and smiled. Blackmail might just work. She found what she had been looking for.

Chapter Nine

Gamble Coulhoon and Major Andrew Stone began their lives in a parallel direction. Both were born to well-to-do families, one to a successful American executive, the other to a highly placed titled British family, long on the title, short on funds. Both entered the military, Gamble during wartime, Stone due to economic necessity, something many second sons of British society were compelled to do. Personal choice directed them to a life of living by their wits, using false identities, traveling the globe, and often placing themselves in danger. One did it for country, the other for personal profit.

Stone finished packing a few personal effects in a large box and slid it over to the door. The building was being watched. He'd seen the men himself. It was time to relocate.

He checked out the window. The three teams were still there. Retreating to a chair, he stopped for a minute to rest. Age was finally catching up. He began berating himself. His whole life was falling apart. For years, he'd enjoyed a lifestyle that most people only dreamed of. Money, wealth, travel. It worked because he had been careful. Careful with whom he did business, careful how he spent his money, careful not to antagonize anyone who could become a potential enemy.

As he sat by the window of the fifth-floor apartment above the Rhinehart Corporation, his mind drifted to the past. For the last fifty years, he had lived a life of the privileged; several beautiful homes, expensive cars, everything that money could buy. Now, he was in trouble. His whole plan was coming apart at the seams. Someone was jeopardizing his world and what to do about it was becoming a major concern. All because of Keegan and his get-rich-quick scheme.

He tried to remember everything about his opponent, but time blurred his memory. He recalled integrity, intelligence, and tenacity. He personally wished no harm to Coulhoon. He hated violence, considering it the weapon of the incompetent, but realized his present business partners possessed no such limitations when threatened. He had to disassociate himself from this whole mess. Maybe there was a way. Perhaps his old friendship with Gamble Coulhoon would prove to be the key.

He was about to leave the apartment when several quiet knocks disrupted his concentration. He walked to the door and tentatively opened it a few inches.

"I need to talk to you," bristled Keegan as he brushed past into the room. "I'm worried about you," he continued. "You look a little green around the gills."

"You needn't concern yourself about me. What are

you doing here? It's dangerous for us to be seen together."

"That's why I came here. I didn't want to use the phone. I was afraid it might be bugged." He pointed to the window. "You got a regular army out there keeping tabs on this place."

"It looks like the police, a private detective, courtesy of Coulhoon and two others. They most likely belong to Harrington. I'm afraid our choice of partners was not well decided."

"It's too late to change our minds now. Look, Stone, we got to keep ahead of the curve here, you know what I mean. We go back a long way and we've had a good run, but things are different now. We gotta bail out of this operation, take our dough and split."

"Are you getting cold feet?"

"It's time. These guys are bad. I don't plan to spend the rest of my life in the slammer, but we gotta go slow. We gotta keep our new partners happy, at least for now and then we can split."

"I'm in total agreement. Perhaps we could leave the network in place. They could buy the gallery and still use it as a drop. Meanwhile, I think we should, how do you say it, lay low. Right now, I have a few things to attend to and we can discuss our next move later." Stone opened the door and checked the hall. It was empty. "Use our special entrance. Under the circumstances, I don't want anyone seeing either of us when we leave."

"Right. I'll be at my place. Call me tonight." Keegan left as quietly as he came.

Stone waited a few minutes before he made his move. Reaching for his coat and umbrella, he took a flashlight from the bookshelf and shoved it into his side pocket.

Knowing the front entrance was under surveillance,

he left the suite with a small attaché case and took the back stairs to the basement. Directing the beam of the flashlight to the wall on his right, he unlocked a metal door connecting to the next building and headed for the stairs. When he reached the top, he eased open the door and checked the hall. It was empty. Donning his raincoat and a wide-brimmed soft hat, he slipped out the outer door into the alley.

The sky opened up. An expected late afternoon shower suddenly turned vicious with a torrential downpour and gusts of powerful winds. Stone raised his umbrella and hurried to the side street, far away from the prying eyes of the unsuspecting men waiting outside his front door.

He walked quickly. The rain worked in his favor, for everyone else was scurrying to avoid the storm. He arrived at his destination, wet, but convinced no one had followed him. In the doorway, an old woman stooped to find the lock, juggling her keys and bags of groceries.

"Here, let me help," he offered as he reached for the bundles. He waited patiently as she inserted the key and pushed open the door.

"Thank you, it's nice to see some people still have some manners," she said, smiling.

"My pleasure," he replied as he followed her inside. He watched as she climbed the stairs, then glanced at the mailboxes to find the right apartment. Waiting until she was safely out of sight, he went in search of 1C.

"I'm surprised it took you this long. Come in," Gamble Coulhoon stepped aside and ushered his guest inside.

"You were expecting me?"

"Let's just say, I'm not surprised." Gamble followed him into the living room. "Let me have your coat and umbrella. I'll hang them in the hall to dry."

Stone stripped off his wet garments and took a few minutes to peruse the tastefully decorated room. He took in the antiques, books and comfortable furniture, all melded together to convey a lived-in atmosphere. But what caught his eye were the paintings on the walls.

"Very nice, but then you always had good taste," he said as his host came back into the room.

"Now I can afford my vices. Paintings have always been my passion." He motioned to a large pale-green easy chair. "Make yourself comfortable while I make us a drink. It is still scotch, neat?"

"You have a good memory."

"I was well trained." He handed Stone a glass and settled in a chair adjacent to him. "Now, tell me why you're here."

"Your newly kindled interest in my affairs is causing me a great deal of trouble."

"Your affairs, as you aptly put it, include the selling of stolen property, artwork that rightfully belongs to people who gave their lives for an unseemly cause."

"That wasn't my doing. I only relieved the true criminals of their ill-gotten goods. I never killed anyone."

"You didn't have anything to do with DeLacroix's death?"

"Violence is not my style, you know that."

"That's what makes this thing so troublesome. Who are you involved with? I have a feeling their philosophy isn't exactly in line with yours."

"Let me ask you something first before I answer that question. Were you always involved with espionage? I mean when we worked together in Paris. I assumed you were just a clerk with an art background."

"I was recruited when I joined the Army. It was a basic operation then, nothing special. When the art collection was discovered, they assigned me to find out what I could; who, what, where, everything. They needed proof for the war crimes trial. My knowledge of the art world was a plus. They could get two jobs done for the price of one."

"And you never suspected what I was up to?"

"Not at the time, but later, after you disappeared, I put two and two together. But I couldn't prove anything nor could I discover your whereabouts. You did an excellent job, I might add."

Stone stood up and walked to the window. "Now, it's all in jeopardy. I spend years assembling this business and it's all slipping through my fingers." He turned to face Gamble. "I did not kill DeLacroix!"

"Then who did? Your new associates?"

"You mean Tim Harrington. I see you've done your homework. He tells me no, but then he'd lie to the Pope if he thought it necessary."

"Why don't you leave town? The police aren't going to give up. Too many people want answers. Harrington is a very big fish. His conviction could make a lot of careers. They want him behind bars and you're going to get caught right in the middle of this tug-of-war."

"It's not that simple. You don't just walk out on a man like that."

"What is his game with you, guns or drugs?"

"That and more. Sometimes it's guns, sometimes cash. Often drugs are used as payment or a swap. Whatever the customer wants. He uses my network as a conduit to help the Irish. He fancies himself as a patriot. He's firmly entrenched in the cause. There are a lot of people who have the same sentiments. Sometimes I can't blame them. We English don't exactly have clean hands."

"All the same, the killing's got to stop," said Gamble. "How involved are you in his activities?"

"I'm not. We share the system, that's all."

"And what about me? Someone's tried to kill me twice in the last couple of weeks."

"I don't think it was Harrington. He was furious when DeLacroix turned up dead in the alley. He doesn't want the police looking into his activities any more than I do."

"Then who did it?"

"I don't know, but I'm trying to find out. Maybe the same person is responsible. I came here with a proposition. This whole arrangement is too dangerous. I'll help you get Harrington, but I want full immunity."

"You'll have to give up everything. The police won't let you continue with your endeavors. They'll confiscate your inventory and shut down your organization."

"I'm willing, as long as I don't go to prison. I made a bad mistake becoming involved with Harrington. I hope to escape with my life."

"I trust you have something tucked away for just such an emergency."

Stone smiled and stood up. "Now I think I've taken enough of your time."

"The police have an all points bulletin out on you."

"I've been evading the authorities on three continents and more than a dozen countries for more than fifty years. I think I can evade arrest for a little while longer."

"They know about the Rhinehart Corporation."

"I guessed that. It can stand the scrutiny. I've already moved my personal things from the premises." Stone headed for the door. "Let's exchange cell phone numbers. That way we can keep each other informed."

"And I won't know where you live."

"Precisely."

The two men exchanged numbers.

"I'll see that your proposal is presented to the proper authorities."

"You won't try to follow me, I trust."

"My word. One gentleman to another." Gamble watched as Stone quietly closed the door. It was useless to follow him and besides, he really didn't want the man caught. In a way, he admired Stone. Anyone who could disappear for fifty years deserved respect. Stone wasn't the murderer and Gamble needed his help.

Chapter Ten

Conlon's first stop of the day was to the Bryson Gallery. Since it was a little after ten, he easily found a parking space. The horde of shoppers had yet to converge on the neighborhood.

He entered the deserted display area and spent a few minutes checking out the paintings on the wall. Some he liked, some he hated and some he dismissed as junk.

After a few minutes, he heard the click of high heels on the hardwood floor and turned to come face-to-face with Elena Lassiter.

"Detective Conlon," she said. "What brings you here? More questions?"

"Isn't it dangerous to leave the door unlocked with no one out here?"

"We have cameras everywhere."

Conlon nodded. "I have a few odds and ends that

need clearing up. I'm a stickler for details." He motioned toward the office. "Could we talk in there?"

"If you like." She led him down the hall and closed the door behind them. "Now, what can I do for you?" She sat at her desk but didn't offer Conlon a chair. He found one anyway.

"Miss Lassiter—"

"It's Elena."

"Ah, Miss Lassiter, we seem to have a problem. It appears you haven't been telling me the truth."

"Nonsense. I've got nothing to hide."

"I guess it slipped your mind that you and Mr. DeLacroix had more than a business relationship."

"I didn't think it important. We were both adults, and unattached I might add. Besides, I didn't want to make it public knowledge."

"Lying to the police could be considered obstruction of justice."

"Oh, get off it." Her cool detachment suddenly disappeared, revealing the long-hidden rough edges of her childhood. She reached for a pack of cigarettes and a lighter. "So we were having a thing, no big deal. Happens all the time." She tapped the pack against the desk, but didn't open it. Then she opened the drawer and put them away.

"How many trips to Europe did you take with him in the last six months?"

"Three. London, Paris, and Switzerland. We visited art galleries owned by the parent company and a few others. We selected inventory, discussed what was to be shown in Boston, and had dinner with a few associates, the usual thing. Why?"

"We believe your boss was involved with a lot more than art. Did he often take large sums of money with him?"

"Of course, the art world loves to deal in cash. No

paper trail. Makes it difficult for the IRS, if you get my drift. Private sales are always going on. Sometimes it's done with money or with a swap. A high-class barter system of sorts."

Conlon eyed her for a moment. "Was anything taken the night Mr. DeLacroix was murdered? Money, artwork?"

"I don't think so. I haven't found anything missing. I already told you people that. You might want to ask my new boss. He's in charge now and has a complete inventory. He's not here at the moment, but if you call later, I'm sure he can squeeze you in."

"I'll catch him another time." She was beginning to annoy him. For a young girl, she was a little too brittle and had a real attitude. He attributed it to nerves. She seemed like a nice kid in a league way over her head.

"Lieutenant, if DeLacroix was mixed up in something illegal, I wasn't involved. We had a few laughs; he bought me a few presents, that's all. Whatever he was into, it wasn't part of my arrangement with him."

"I appreciate your candor. If you come across anything, give me a call." He handed her a business card and left.

Elena waited until she was sure he had left the building, then turned on her computer. She scanned the latest inventory lists and quickly directed the cursor to the print icon. She was about finished when the buzzer announced someone entering the gallery. Looking at the closed circuit television monitor, she spied her new boss, Eric Tyler, making his way back to the office. She cancelled out the program, grabbed the sheets from the printer tray and placed them under the files on her desk. It wasn't the safest place to hide them, but she was afraid the security cameras would show her trying to conceal them. She reached for the phone as he came through the door.

"Good morning, Mr. Tyler." She smiled, trying to control her voice. After all, he was her next target.

"Miss Lassiter," he replied perfunctorily. "Did I see a customer leaving the building?"

"I had a visit from the police. They're still investigating the murder. I'm afraid they don't have any clues."

Tyler busied himself with the mail. "Shouldn't you be out front?"

"I'm expecting a small shipment from Paris. It's a few days overdue. I was trying to track it on the Internet. It's not important, I can do it later."

"No, finish what you're doing. I'll be in my office if you need me."

Breathing a sigh of relief, she watched him disappear behind a closed door. The blinking light on the desk extension caught her attention. Tyler was making a call. She opened the bottom drawer of her desk, reached for a bag containing a couple of donuts, and placed then on the desk. Then she walked to a long sideboard on the far wall and poured a cup of coffee. She returned to the desk and pretended to enjoy her forced morning break.

She checked the extension. The light was still on. He was still using the phone. She turned the computer back on and continued a quick search of the files. It was full of new data. Too much to print out at the office. It was something she could deal with later. She returned the computer to its desktop mode and slipped the hidden printed pages in the bottom drawer, placing the paper bag with the uneaten donut on top. Finishing the last of the coffee, she went out on the gallery floor and waited for Tyler to leave.

Fifteen minutes later, he came out of his office and barely stopped long enough to tell her he was leaving and wouldn't be back for the rest of the day. Something had spooked him.

She closed the gallery at six and locked the front door. Back in the office, she turned off the security camera. For the next thirty minutes, she used the modem and transferred the inventory files and De-Lacroix's personal data to her home computer. It was a lot safer than the copy machine.

She knew the danger, but it was her ticket out. Her dreams didn't include a life of quiet desperation. When she finished, she turned the camera back on, set the security code and left the building, praying no one would notice the time lapse on the security film. One phone call and she could be set for life.

Donna and Bob arrived at Jennifer's office after five with their reports and they went into the conference room. The law offices were nearly empty. Only a few young associates short of monthly billable hours remained. No one paid much attention to them.

"Thanks for coming here. I seem to be having a time management problem lately." She sat at the head of the table and waited while they organized their notes.

"I skipped most of the personal background on DeLacroix," said Donna. "I took it for granted you already knew it. There was something, though." She searched through her papers until she found the one she wanted. "His ex-wife. She controls the money, even now. He received a salary and paid alimony and child support, but she was in charge of their investments. They weren't divided when they were divorced."

"Maybe he wasn't very good with money and trusted her."

"Would you trust your ex-wife to handle your money?" asked Jennifer.

"Seems odd, so I did a little more research. She came to the marriage with all the assets. Everything they had began with her money. He either didn't have a prayer of getting any of it or he wanted out so badly, he was willing to leave it behind. I still don't have the answer."

"That rules out the wife. Obviously, she didn't need him."

"The waterfront condo is leased to a corporation. It's all legally filed with the State House, but he's the only officer. Money is deposited every month and a check pays the rent and parking fee. Elena pays the utilities. Aside from that, he's clean. No big debts, no gambling, nothing. His only vice seems to be the young lady."

"What about the Rhinehart Corporation?"

"That's me," said Bob. "It's just what Stone said, a legitimate import–export company that deals in art. It has all the proper licenses and there is no record at the Better Business Bureau of any complaints. Sorry."

"I was hoping, but—"

"There was one more thing. It concerns Keegan. His family never applied for his death benefits from the Army. It wasn't much, but that seems strange. You'd think they could have used the money."

"Maybe he's alive and they know it."

It was nearly ten o'clock and Conlon was about to leave his office when the call came in.

"Lieutenant, just got the call. The doorman at some fancy condo down by the Aquarium just found one of the tenants dead. The Captain said I should I tell you. Says it might be related to one of your cases."

Conlon heaved a deep sigh. The address stirred his memory. "Tell them I'm on my way."

Fifteen minutes later, with the blue light blinking, he pulled his car into the private lot of the condo and parked close to the building. He barely noticed the noise and confusion, for it was now a common sight to him.

"Where?" he asked the uniform at the door.

"Fourth floor, Lieutenant. A young one this time, pretty too. Such a waste."

Only one officer greeted him as he stepped off the elevator. "Where is everyone?" he asked.

"On their way. I guess it's a busy night. She's in the bedroom."

Conlon stepped inside and looked around the living room. It was a mess, a far cry from the last time he had been there. The place had been ransacked. Cushions dotted the carpet. The upholstery fabric on the couch and chairs was shredded. Lamps lay tilted on their sides and every drawer was turned out. It looked like a markdown table in Filene's Bargain Basement, where every Bostonian often shopped.

He stepped around the clutter and entered the bedroom. It was the same. The bed was torn apart and the victim's clothes lay in shreds on the floor. Elena Lassiter's body lay face-down on the carpet. A thin trickle of red followed a path to a large pool of blood, still wet and shiny, surrounding her head. He moved closer and knelt by the body. He touched her skin. It was still warm. He checked the wound. It seemed so small. *How could such a tiny hole cause so much damage,* he thought. *It was such a waste.*

He slowly got to his feet as the forensics crew arrived and began their orderly collection of clues. For some reason, he wanted to leave. He felt tightness in his chest and a bad taste filled his mouth. He went back into the living room and looked out the window at Boston Harbor. Everything looked so clean and peaceful. What he really wanted to do was leave. For some reason, this one was having a bad effect on his nerves.

He gave the room another look. There was so much chaos; it was impossible to make a search. One thing did catch his eye. Her computer. It was on. Maybe there would be a clue hidden in the maze of information, but all that was beyond his comprehension. He made a mental note to get an expert to check it out.

Deciding not to wait for a preliminary report, he took the elevator to the ground floor. The assigned detectives were standing in the lobby. "Do the usual and have the report on my desk tomorrow. I'll be in first thing in the morning." As he walked to his car, he checked his watch. It was nearly eleven. Instead of heading home, he made a detour to Jennifer's address, arriving at her door a few minutes later.

"You don't look exactly great," she offered as she let him into the apartment.

"I'm not. I've just come from Elena Lassiter's apartment. Someone decided to put a bullet in her brain."

"Dear heaven. Gamble's here. I was just about to make coffee."

"I heard your conversation," said Gamble. "She was just a child. What kind of people are we dealing with?"

"I'm afraid to think about it." Conlon took off his coat, leaving it on the back of a chair. He went to the window, too tense to sit. "Obviously, Miss Lassiter found out something that was so damaging they had to shut her up. Maybe she was trying to blackmail them, I don't know." He finally collapsed on a chair. "She wasn't really a bad kid."

"What could be so important that two people had to be murdered?" asked Jennifer.

"I may have some insight into this," offered Gamble. "I met with the Major today."

"You two are a perfect pair. The whole world is looking for this guy and you two meet with him like it's no big deal. I'm surprised he hasn't invited you for cocktails." He threw up his hands in disgust. "I'm sorry, but this thing is getting to me. Tell me what happened."

"He arrived at my apartment totally unannounced. We had a long conversation. He said he didn't kill DeLacroix and I believe him."

"What about Harrington?" asked Conlon.

"Stone admitted he's in business with Harrington, but knows he made a mistake. He wants to make a deal. He'll help us with Harrington for full immunity."

"He doesn't want much, does he?"

"He could land that thief for you."

"I'll have to go to the Chief. He might go for it. What else did you and your long-lost pal talk about?"

"The rundown on the last fifty years of his life."

"Must be fascinating," said Jennifer.

"I learned quite a lot. They put together a beautiful arrangement. Keegan found two men who were willing, for a price, to transport the goods to a warehouse in Marseilles. Then, they found a small cheap hotel and stayed hidden until the police stopped looking.

"Stone found an old rundown isolated chateau in Avignon where they moved the paintings. They stored the collection in the cellars and sat on the goods for more than two years. It was a perfect storage area, cool and dry and they were all properly crated, thanks to the Army. He sold several pieces of jewelry, the gems, separately and had the settings melted down. I'm sure he regretted that. Some of them were exceptional works of art, but it would have been too risky to sell them intact. They lived off the proceeds for quite some time.

"Stone made extensive renovations to the place, including electricity and plumbing. Everything was in deplorable condition. He even has a climate-controlled display room where he hangs them. They're still in excellent condition."

Gamble smiled. "They began selling the paintings a few at a time, mostly to private collectors. You'd be surprised how the rich enjoy a little larceny. They're willing to pay enormous prices.

"By the middle fifties, they developed several contacts in the art world and built a credible reputation. Auction houses were particularly helpful. Most never cared where he got the merchandise; their only interest was profit. Europe was in chaos. Records had disappeared. It was a perfect milieu. To cover himself, he bought other works and formed a legitimate business, The Rhinehart Corporation. He even paid taxes like every other honest citizen. As to the present murders, he doesn't think Harrington is involved."

"I'm sure Harrington's got an iron-clad alibi, but he could have ordered the hits," said Conlon.

"Doesn't make sense." Jennifer returned to the conversation with a pot of coffee and three cups. "He's got a good thing going. Why would he want to draw attention to it?"

"Stone agrees. He's also terrified. His whole life is coming apart. At this point, I don't think he knows who to trust. We've exchanged cell phone numbers. If he comes across anything, he's promised to call."

"And you believe that rot?"

Gamble nodded. "I do. He wants a deal. He said something else. There are three surveillance teams stationed outside the Rhinehart building."

"Three. We've got one and Brian has one, but who's the third?"

"Stone thinks it's Harrington. Now do you see why I believe him? Oh, by the way. He's not there anymore. He gave everyone the slip."

Andrew Stone was frightened. As he entered Harrington's pub, his mind was a swirl of ideas and fantasies, all of them bad. His past business associates at least portrayed a facade of manners and sophistication, but his new present partner had no regard for property or human life. All he wanted was results.

The building appeared to be at least a hundred years old. The benches were worn and the stools battered and gouged, all illuminated by very poor lighting. The bar itself shone with a patina of years of rubbing and polishing. A huge scratched gilt-framed mirror, distorting the shabby surroundings, supplied the backdrop to the well-stocked shelves behind the bar. Three ancient fans made a feeble attempt to circulate the smoke. There was no enforcement of the clean air act here. This was a working-class bar, a neighborhood institution where ordinary people with all the usual problems occupied the booths and warmed the tattered green leather seats at the bar.

He could feel every stare and hear the murmur of comments as he passed through the room to the back of the building. He most definitely did not belong. Knocking at the office door, he waited impatiently for it to be opened. His stomach tensed as he crossed the threshold.

The room was much the same as the pub: old, worn, and drab. Tim Harrington was at his desk. A couple of his henchmen sat sprawled in two oversized chairs near the only window. "I have a very big problem, Stone, and I hope you're not the cause."

"If you're referring to the murder . . ."

"Murders, Stone. That girl, the one who worked at the gallery, someone knocked her off. You know anything about it?"

"You don't think—"

"I don't think anything. I want to know what's going on here. All this is bad for business. Find someone that we can trust to replace her. I need that gallery as a front."

"I seem to have a problem of my own," replied Stone. "Why are you having me followed?"

"What are you talking about?"

"The police and some private detective that Mc-Callum has on her payroll have been outside my apartment for the last few days. Now, there's more. I assumed they were your men."

"Not mine." Harrington was obviously surprised by the news. "This thing is getting out of hand. I may not be happy about what's going on, but I got no real beef with you, yet. But if I find out you're lying to me, then we will have a problem."

"That's comforting to know." Stone swallowed the bile in his throat and tried not to look intimidated. "I think we should discontinue our little arrangement for a while. It's too dangerous."

"Major, it's not that simple. I've made promises to people and they expect results. They don't like excuses."

"But surely, if they knew what a predicament we're in, they would understand."

"Wake up and smell the coffee. They expect me to deliver and don't care about my problems. Do you get my drift?"

"Unfortunately, yes. I would like to offer you a proposition. Why don't you take over my route, for a small remuneration? That way I could take an early retirement. Things are getting too complicated. I'm not sure I want to be part of them."

"I'll think about it. Meanwhile, find a place to lay low for a while. I'll take care of things at my end. I can hold off my associates for a while, so take a breather. When the cops lose interest, we can go back into business. I'll have one of the boys take you where you want to go. It will be safer that way."

Stone left the pub with the bodyguards and climbed into the car. Sweat poured down his neck and back as he envisioned a cold wet grave in Boston Harbor, his feet tied to a block of cement. He was amazed when they dropped him off near his destination, a small out-of-the-way hotel near the Fleet Center.

When he reached his room, he immediately made a call to Keegan. "Harrington says he's not having me followed."

"And you believe the guy? If it's not the cops and not the lady lawyer and not him, then who is it? Who else would want to have you tailed?"

"I can't imagine."

"My point. Then it has to be Harrington. You can't trust the guy. Where are you?"

"At a small place near The Fleet Center. It's out of the way, but well appointed."

"This is no time for you to be worrying about what the place looks like. Get with the program, Major, we're in real trouble here. Stay out of sight for a while and don't talk to anybody. Let me see what I can find out. Call me in a couple of days."

Stone hung up the receiver and stretched out on the bed. He tried to take a nap, but visions of iron bars and worse kept streaking through his imagination. He propped the pillows against the headboard and put his mind to work. After a few minutes, he picked up the phone and dialed.

*   *   *

Atkins and Klein spent the morning canvassing the area surrounding Elena Lassiter's condo. Since there was no doorman, they began knocking on the doors of the other owners in the building. As usual, no one saw anything. Then, they hit pay dirt. As they left the building, Atkins spotted the parking attendant in the public lot next to the building. They stepped over the small fence and walked up to the gatehouse that controlled the entrance.

"Were you here last night?" Atkins asked, flashing his badge.

"Yeah, you guys on that homicide thing?"

Atkins nodded. "Did you see anything or anyone hanging around the building over there?"

"Come to think of it, yeah. The girl came home around eight. She was a real looker; you know what I mean. Anyway, she waved to me. Sometimes, I watch her car if she goes out of town for a few days. Nice kid. Too bad."

"Could you get to the point?"

"Sorry. She goes inside and a little while later, these two guys, one young, one old, come into the lot and park their car, a nice red job, one of them muscle cars. The older guy leaves me the key, pays the ten bucks and they go over to the building, press the buzzer and go in."

"I take it they don't live there."

"Nah. I seen one of them a couple of times. One time, he and another guy dropped her off. It was pretty late."

Atkins was showing his impatience. "What happened last night?"

"They stay in there for about an hour, come out, get into the car and drive away."

"What time was that?"

"Sometime after eleven, the news had just come on."

"The news?" asked Klein.

"Yeah, I got a little TV in here. The wife, she give it to me for my birthday. That way I can watch the Celtics. Love the game."

"What do these guys look like?"

"The older one, not too tall, thin, kinda old, maybe in his seventies. Had on a dark jacket. Wore glasses."

"And the other?"

"Same size, maybe thirty-five, looked like they might be related. You know, the same look."

"Do you have his parking stub?"

"Got it here, somewhere, wait a minute, but there's no license plate number on it, only make, date and time. We don't do that no more." The stubs were separated into small compartments, one for each day. "Here it is. We weren't very busy that night."

Klein opened a small plastic bag. "Drop it in here. If your boss gives you any grief, tell him it's evidence in a murder trial. We may have to have you come downtown for a statement."

"No problem. Always happy to help you guys."

Chapter Eleven

Major Stone walked slowly through the center aisle of the Quincy Market food court, nibbling on a small batch of fried clams. It was early evening. The happy hour crowd and serious diners were searching for empty tables in the restaurants that occupied the two glass-enclosed outer areas that paralleled the main building. Others, like him, meandered through the main building sampling every type of food from pizza to sushi.

He strolled outside and found an empty bench in the courtyard separating the three buildings that comprised one of the most popular shopping areas in the city. Dark shadows spread across the bricks, but there was enough light for him to still see his surroundings. Munching on his snack, he waited. Five minutes later, he had company.

"I wasn't expecting you to bring anyone," he said, displaying a spark of anger.

"I wanted Jennifer here so she could hear our conversation. I understand you two have already met."

"I'm not sure I like this, but you don't give me much choice."

"Major Stone—" said Jennifer.

"Please call me Andrew. The title *Major* disappeared a long time ago."

"Andrew. Gamble is in a lot of trouble. The police are being pressured for an arrest and at this moment, he's their only suspect. What can you tell us that will help find the real murderer?"

"Very little, I'm afraid. It's all so confusing. Neither Harington nor I want all this attention. He's convinced me that he's not the culprit, but then he's not the most honest of men. It must be some outside party, but I have no idea who or why. Believe me, my dear, if I knew anything, I'd tell you. My very existence is at stake here."

"Tell me about The Rhinehart Corporation."

"It's a legitimate venture. We broker art for many people."

"There's a third team watching the building. Do you have any idea who they are?"

"No, I thought they belonged to Harrington, but he says no. It won't do them any good. I've vacated the premises for a safer haven, at least for the present."

"Do you think you could get close to them without being seen? If you could recognize them, it would be a great help," urged Jennifer.

"I must admit I've become quite good at this disguise thing. I doubt they'll spot me. Yes, I'll give it a try."

"Great. You can reach us through Gamble's cell phone. And please be careful."

"I don't advocate violence, young lady. Stealing is one thing, but killing is another. I hope you believe me." He got up, shook hands with Gamble and tipped his hat to Jennifer as he walked away, blending into the crowd.

"Now what?" she asked.

"We see if he can be trusted."

"We do?"

"Not you, Marko and I. Leave this part to us."

The next morning Gamble and Marko positioned themselves just inside the subway station down the block from the Rhinehart Corporation. It afforded them an excellent observation point along with the added camouflage of the morning commuter traffic.

"The police team is in the coffee shop and Brian is in the white van parked near the corner," said Gamble. "Our third party is in that black car on the other side of the street."

"Give me the license plate number. I'll have my friend at the Registry run it." Marko pulled out a pad and jotted it down as Gamble recited it. Using his cell phone, he called in the plate and hung up. "She'll call us back in a few minutes."

"She?"

"She's an old acquaintance and dear friend, nothing more. Where's Stone?"

"He's on the corner, sitting on that bench, reading the paper. He's quite good. Look at his disguise. Different clothes, a wig, simple, but effective. I must commend him next time we meet."

They waited for more than an hour until a relief man changed places with his accomplice in the black car. Marko's car phone rang as the first man walked away. It was his friend at the DMV. They exchanged a few words and he hung up.

"The car is a rental, probably from the airport."

"That's a dead end. Look, Stone's leaving. Maybe

he'll have something for us. Let's go, mission accomplished, I hope."

Conlon stood waiting when Jennifer emerged from the courthouse. "You don't look too happy," she offered as they moved out of the line of traffic.

"It's Mancuso. Someone tipped him about your interest in the murder investigations."

"Don't tell me he's going to take a personal interest in this mess?"

"Not quite, but he's assigned Tony Romano to look into it."

"That useless bag of wind will have his nose everywhere and then he'll go running to the DA with a full report every morning. He'll do anything to follow in Mancuso's footsteps. This calls for a little personal stroking."

"Tony hates you."

"Not him, the big man himself. At least we have respect for each other. Tony is another matter. He makes my skin crawl. The public sector is full of yes men like him and I don't have time to deal with them."

She thought for a moment. "The pressure must be on. This means a visit to the lion's den. Maybe I can buy us some time."

"Mancuso needs a big case. And he still can't deal with the idea that that you deserted his ship when he needed you most. He's got his own agenda and if he can use you as a doormat, he will. Be careful."

"I'll talk to you later and thanks for the heads-up." She walked back into the courthouse, hoping to find the District Attorney somewhere in the building. A casual meeting would be better than a formal appointment. She spent a few minutes searching the halls and was about to give up when she spotted him walking in her direction, head down, reading a file. She stepped up her pace and caught up with him as he reached the elevator.

"Anthony," she said casually.

"Jennifer. I didn't notice your name on the docket today."

She knew he kept a running tally on the major cases under his tutelage. "Just some preliminary things, nothing important. I would like to talk to you if you have a few minutes."

He glanced at his watch. "If we can keep it brief." They moved away from the crowd to a nearby window. "What can I do for you?"

"It's about the DeLacroix murder investigation. A little bird told me you're taking a personal interest in it."

"Ah, yes. It's fast becomming an embarrassment to the Department. The Chief has asked me to keep a close eye on the proceedings."

"And my involvement hasn't colored your thinking?"

"Off the record, it would be my pleasure to humiliate you in public, but not at the expense of the county. You're not thinking of backing the wrong horse this time?"

"Gamble Coulhoon's one of my oldest and dearest friends, Tony, and no he didn't do it. I just need a little time to prove it."

"Understood, but don't take too long."

Jennifer picked up Gamble outside the university's front entrance on Commonwealth Avenue and drove to Brookline, one of Boston's most expensive suburbs. They had an appointment with Sarah Gerwitz, the owner of the paintings in question. They parked under the shade of one of the many huge oak trees that lined the quiet street, then knocked on the door of a large brick Tudor-style house. The maid opened the door and led them into an expensively decorated formal living room. Both paintings hung on the wall.

When she joined them, Sarah found Gamble closely examining the frames. "You never let go."

"Sarah." Gamble greeted his host with a warm hug. He introduced the two women to each other, then looked back at the paintings. "I'd like you to tell Jennifer their history right up to recent events."

Jennifer noticed an extra twinkle in Gamble's eye. Obviously, this woman was more than a passing acquaintance. She had to admire his taste in women. Though Sarah Gerwitz was in her seventies, she was still striking. It wasn't that she was beautiful, it was the way she dressed and carried herself; with the flair of a woman in total control. Jennifer found herself a bit envious. Maybe she'd acquire that quality when she reached Sarah's age.

Their hostess directed them to same comfortable chairs by the fireplace and began her story. "My parents were German Jews living in Munich. Before the war, they were both doctors, came from wealthy families and were very active in the community, especially the arts.

"My father saw the writing on the wall in 1936 and sent my brother and me to England, supposedly for our education, but it was really to get us out of the country. We carried most of my mother's jewelry sewn in the linings of our clothes. On a subsequent trip to visit us, my mother smuggled the paintings out in the false bottom of a suitcase.

"In 1938, all communication was cut off. We received a letter from a Christian neighbor informing us that my parents had been arrested and sent to one of the camps. I never found out which one. We never saw them again." She paused for a moment, but there were no tears. "Forgive me, it happened a long time ago, but it's still a painful memory."

Jennifer couldn't think of anything to say. A vision of her father and mother kept fleeting in and out of her thoughts. *What if it had happened to them?* All she could do was nod her head.

"When I came to Washington for my graduate studies, I brought the paintings with me. I met David, my late husband, when he worked for your father."

"Seems as though everyone worked for my father at one time or another."

Sarah smiled. "One night at a party in our home, Gamble noticed them and told me of his suspicions. He's been on a quest to find their mates ever since. He's told me what's been happening. I'll be happy to help you any way I can."

"Has anyone approached you, perhaps offering to buy them?"

"Tell her about the attempted robbery," said Gamble.

"About a month ago, I went to visit my brother who teaches at Columbia. I gave my housekeeper the time off so she could visit her family in England. When I got back, I found the alarm system had been turned off."

"What was taken?"

"That's the strange part. Nothing was even disturbed, but the police found a broken window in the back."

"And the paintings?"

"They were in the vault at the bank. I always secure them along with my jewelry and silver when the house is empty."

"Who knows about the paintings?"

"I've never kept them a secret. Anyone who's been a guest in my house knows about them as well as a great many art dealers. Alone, they're not terribly valuable, but four together, well that's another matter."

Gamble took one of the paintings from the wall and began examining it closely. He paid particular attention to the frames. "Now that I've seen them again, I'm sure the frames on the pictures on the gallery are similar, but not the same."

"What are you getting at?"

"I'm not sure." He reached for the second painting and placed it next to the first. "These frames are exactly the same, as exact as two handmade can be. Look at the scrollwork and the gold overlay. The same artisan did them. The others in the gallery are thinner and the workmanship not as good, nor as exact. Somehow, I've got to see the other paintings again." He hung the artwork back on the wall. "Thank you, Sarah. You've been a great help."

"Don't forget dinner on Friday."

"Never. But now, we have work to do."

Jennifer hardly had time to say good-bye before Gamble pushed her out the door. "What are you up to?" she asked when they reached the car.

"I'm not sure, but I think we've uncovered a lot more than a stolen art ring. Drive to your father's. I need help from an expert."

"And Sarah Gerwitz?"

"She's an old dear friend and that's all you need to know."

They arrived at the Beacon Hill house a short time later and found Brand McCallum in the library, reading. "Ah, my favorite daughter and her new partner in crime."

"Your only daughter, Dad, and we need your help."

Gamble joined her on the couch. "I don't think Stone is selling stolen art, I think he's keeping the originals and palming forgeries. We just came from seeing two real ones and their frames are not quite the same as the ones I saw in the gallery."

"Unless you get the four of them together, it will be difficult to prove."

"Let's dangle a carrot in front of our supposed new gallery owner. Donna and Bob are scheduled to go back there tomorrow. What if they call early and insinuate that they're ready to make a deal only if all four paintings can be produced for examination. If they're offered the two that belong to Sarah, someone will have to steal them. If they produce all four without making any contact with her, then we'll know they're selling forgeries. What do you think?" Gamble sat back, quite pleased with his scenario.

"Dangerous, it's too dangerous for civilians," said Brand. "You know how I feel about using the untrained."

"I'll run it by Conlon and see what he thinks," promised Jennifer.

"If he agrees, maybe then, but be careful, this could all blow up in your face, but if you succeed, you might just solve all your problems."

"I will, Dad, I promise."

"Does this new gallery owner know you, Gamble?" Brand asked.

"I don't think so, why?"

"Perhaps you could tag along as their art expert. That way you could examine them firsthand and get a feel for the situation. We're dealing with several unknown dangerous entities and nothing will ever replace the instincts of an experienced agent."

"It's worth taking a shot." He got up to leave. "Come Jennifer, we've had a long day."

"I'll call you tomorrow, Dad."

"Come back to the house and I'll make some dinner," she offered as they got into the car.

"Forgive me, Jennifer, but your talents don't lie in the kitchen. Why don't we pick up some Chinese."

"I guess I'll never be a chef." She pulled her phone from the console separating the two front seats and handed it to Gamble. "Ling Ho is on my speed dial."

As they pulled into the alley behind Jennifer's building, she noticed the opened door leading to her back stairs. Stopping the car, she grabbed the phone and entered the building. She climbed the stairs two at a time to her third-floor living area and stopped. The door was open. She ran back down the stairs and called 911. "We better wait here."

Five minutes later, a cruiser drove into the alley and stopped behind her car. Two officers attacked the stairs. She started to follow, but Gamble stopped her. "They don't need you up there."

A few minutes later, the officers returned. "Whoever it was is gone. You can go up. It's pretty much of a mess, I'm afraid," one said. "Let us know if anything's been stolen."

"Thanks." She handed Gamble her briefcase and the bag of food, then moved the car to her parking space. By the time she returned, Gamble had the cartons out of the bag and the plates on the counter. She looked into the living room.

"Don't go in there. We can tackle it later."

"That bad?"

"The young policewoman wasn't exaggerating."

"What do you think they were looking for?"

"My guess, my copy of the art collection list. They didn't find it at my place, so they took a chance on yours."

"What about my computer?"

"Still intact. Of course, we won't know if they deleted anything until you turn it on."

"I copied the information on my hard drive, but hid the disk in my office safe. We're covered." She began opening the cartons and spooning out the food. "These people aren't pulling any punches."

"There's a great deal at stake. When people feel threatened, they're unpredictable and dangerous. From now on, we have to be even more careful."

Chapter Twelve

Conlon entered the morgue and found Barbara Washington stripping off her greens. The strong smell of chemicals permeated the air. "Let's get out of here," she said. "I know how you hate this place."

Conlon followed her down the hall to her office. "What's so important that you beeped me? Good news, I hope."

"Better than good, Conlon. I sent the bullets that killed the Lassiter girl to forensics and asked to have them compare it to the one that killed the art dealer. They came from the same gun."

Conlon sat for a minute, tapping his fists together. "Anything else?"

"You guys are never satisfied and yes, there is something else. There were several bruises on her body. Looks like the killer slapped her around and her clothes were torn. He must have straightened her up after she died."

"Was she sexually assaulted?"

"No, that wasn't the deal. I think he needed some answers and she was either not willing or unable to tell him what he wanted. So, he terrorized her. She went down fighting. We found some skin under her nails and some fibers on her clothes and on one of the chairs. Wool, tweed, brown, probably from a jacket."

"Expensive?"

"Not really, but not cheap, probably off the rack in some fairly decent department store. I'll have a full report on your desk by the end of the day. Hope it helps."

"It may not help to find the perp, but it might eliminate some of the suspects. Thanks, Barbara."

"Anytime. Oh, and I could use some more tea."

Conlon gave her a nod, left the building, and drove to Jennifer's townhouse, hoping to find her at home. When he arrived, he was met with a surprise. Not only was she there, but Brian, Donna, Bob and Gamble were sitting on her tiny balcony.

"Looks like I've walked in on a little pow-wow. What are you up to? No, strike that. I've got something to say first." He grabbed a folding chair from against the wall and joined the group.

"The medical examiner says the same gun that killed DeLacroix killed Elena Lassiter and that she was beaten before she was shot. Now do you see why I don't want any of you playing detective?" He looked at each of them, hoping they were listening. "Now, it's your turn."

"We've got a new plan of action," offered Jennifer.

"We?" he asked as he surveyed the group. "All of you?"

"Gamble thinks Stone is selling forgeries and keeping the real ones," she continued.

"That's original. I'll bite, why?"

Gamble told him about Sarah Gerwitz and their new scheme.

"I don't like it. It's too dangerous. These people have two killings under their belt. A few more won't bother them one bit."

"I'm going with them," said Gamble, "and Brian will be outside in the van."

"Am I supposed to go along with this? I don't think so."

"The police can't do it. By the time you deal with all the red tape, it might be too late. This way, at least we'll know what they're up to. Then you can take it from there."

Conlon exhaled an exasperated sigh. "I give up. Go in there, examine the paintings and find out how much he wants for them. Tell him you need to think about the price and you'll get back to him. Then get out. If we want to make this stick, we have to do it legally." He turned to Bob and Donna. "Make the call. Let's see what the man has to say."

The next morning Bob and Gamble, with Donna wired for sound, entered the Bryson Gallery. Eric Taylor greeted them at the door. Donna introduced Gamble as their art expert and Tyler led them to his office. Leaning against the back wall were the four paintings.

"Where did you get all four?" gasped Donna

"When you indicated interest in the entire group, I began a search for the missing two. Actually, we knew of the existence prior to your inquiry. They were featured with pictures in an auction catalogue dating back to the thirties that I found in the files. So, I tried the Internet. An art dealer in Amsterdam stumbled upon them a few days ago and e-mailed the information as soon as he read my message. They were express delivered yesterday."

He touched one of the paintings, gently trailing his fingers along the top of the frame. "Of course, they're on loan. If we can't come to a meeting of the minds, I'll either have to buy them myself or return them. It would be such a shame to separate them again."

Gamble moved closer and examined each one carefully. All four frames matched, but narrower than the originals. He nodded imperceptibly to Donna. It was her turn to go to work.

"Mr. Tyler, while our friend examines the paintings, why don't you show Bob and I around the gallery. We're not usually interested in contemporary pieces, but there are one or two items that caught my eye." She attached herself to his arm and led him out to the gallery.

Gamble removed a small camera from his pocket and took several shots of each picture, paying close attention to the frames. He finished in a matter of minutes and tucked the camera into his jacket pocket. He was deep into his examination when they returned.

"These are brilliant!" he exclaimed on his best-affected British accent. "I really think you should consider them."

"What do you think would be a fair price for all four of them?" asked Bob.

"I don't think we could consider anything under one hundred thousand, American."

Donna looked to Gamble as though she was seeking an opinion.

"I'm sure Mr. Tyler wouldn't be offended if we took a day or so to think about it."

"As long as you don't take too long. Once it's known that the pieces have been reunited, I'm confident we'll have many other interested parties."

"Of course," Donna replied as she gathered her belongings. "This is Wednesday. Why don't we say, by Monday, you'll have our answer."

They left the gallery and walked down the street. Brian picked them up two blocks away from the building.

"Got every word, right here," he said pointing to the recorder. "Jennifer may not be able to use it in court, but now we know we're on the right trail." He pulled over to the curb in front of a one-hour photo lab where Gamble dropped off the film.

"In my office," said Conlon as he walked past his two best detectives. "We may have a break," he continued.

"We could sure use one."

"Forensics says that the same gun killed DeLacroix and the Lassiter girl."

Atkins let out a low whistle. "What have we got here?"

"I'm not sure. Ask the lab to check the bullets against any unsolved murders in the last five years that involved shootings. Maybe our guy has been around before. Also, there were some fibers underneath her nails. Get the report and see if they can narrow it down. I want to know how expensive the fabric is and who uses it."

"One more thing," said Atkins. "The lab lifted three sets of prints from that parking stub. They're running them through the system now. The attendant is coming in to give the sketch artist a description. I think we've got something."

"At last, progress."

"Come on Klein, let's get to it. Everyone seems to think police work is all high-tech, but in the end, it all comes down to old-fashioned legwork."

* * *

Looking for answers, Conlon headed down the hall
to the hastily arranged temporary office of Pete Etting,
the resident police department computer guru. Conlon
needed quick answers and wanted him away from any
distractions. Knocking on the door, he went inside.

Pete was hunched over his keyboard, thinking out
loud, working his way through the maze of complicated files buried in the hard drive of Elena Lassiter's
PC. A genius with computers, he held a master's de-
gree from MIT and the politics of ambition had no
room in his life. Dressed in chinos, a faded gray sweatshirt, and dirty sneakers, a decent wardrobe was not
high on his list of priorities.

He motioned to Conlon and pointed to the only
other chair in the tiny room. "Give me one more minute," he said as his eyes scanned the screen. "I think
I have what you want." Conlon took a seat and waited
quietly. This was no time for conversation.

"You're gonna love me, Conlon."

"Tell me what you found and this time in English.
No computer garbage, it goes right over my head."

Etting waited a few seconds for the screen to change
its display. "I'll make it as simple as I can, but you
know, you really need to take a class in computers. It
would make life a lot easier."

"Etting, I could take a thousand classes and it
wouldn't do me any good. Now, what have you got?"

"Unlike you, it seems that Miss Lassiter knew her
way around this little baby. She downloaded everything from DeLacroix's business computer to her own
personal one at home. I didn't find a floppy in her
apartment, so she must have transferred it over the
phone."

"Floppy?"

He held up a blank disk. "Like this. Don't tell me
you don't know what these are."

"I know what they are." He had a vague knowledge of what they were used for, but didn't have a clue how they worked. "How do you know the stuff came from his machine?"

"I had a little trouble with his password, but I remembered something. When I picked up his computer, there were some old posters of Tyrone Power movies hanging on the walls, so I plugged in the names and guess what. Zorro. The guy used it as his password. I went through all his files first." He pointed to a computer on the table by the window. "That's DeLacroix's computer. Lots of stuff has been erased, but there's always a way to find it. I matched it up to the files on hers and bingo. Some of it isn't important, but I printed it anyway. You might find something interesting there."

"I thought you said it was erased."

"Even though a file is erased, it still remains on the hard drive. You just have to know where to look." He scrolled down the screen and continued. "Here's a list of sales going back nearly fifty years, a little over two hundred of them. They're all numbered in some kind of code. When I tried to get into one special file, I ran into a roadblock. I guessed it held the key. Your victim must have been paranoid."

"Etting, get to the point. I'd like to know the answer before the millennium becomes history."

"Sorry. Anyway, he used another password. I racked my brain trying to think like the guy and bingo, I found it. Don Diego. Get it?"

"No."

"That's Zorro's real name. Anyway, the whole thing opened up. I found it. Such a great feeling. Take a look."

Conlon leaned closer to the screen as Etting began explaining.

"Here's an example. There's a number at the beginning of every sale. Number nineteen fifty-three with a seven in parentheses. I'm assuming that's the year and the month. Next to it is a name, Sarah Masterson, then the address and price, seventy-five thousand. I don't know what the last entry is, maybe the name of the painting or the artist. I don't recognize any of them, but then I don't know anything about art."

"I know someone who does. Did you find all this stuff in her computer too?"

"Yeah. That's why I know she took it from his computer. She downloaded most of it the same day she was murdered. Coincidence? Maybe. I'm no cop, but I don't think so."

"How would the killer know when and if she did it?"

"If he knows anything about computers, he could tell when she accessed the file. The general files on the office computer were opened almost every day, that's to be expected. But the file with the code was only opened sporadically, usually once at the end of the month. But last week, after DeLacroix was murdered, it was opened several times, all after hours. It was also opened on the day Lassiter was killed. It's all recorded on a separate file."

"If the killer knew the file had been accessed, why didn't he take it out of her computer?"

"He did, at least he thought he did, but when you delete a file, you have to do it in more than one place. Maybe he's not that computer savvy and doesn't know how to do it or maybe he didn't have time to complete the job. I found it on her hard drive. She must have made a copy, but I couldn't find it. I'm guessing the killer took it."

"What about the rest of the stuff?"

"There's a lot of activity in the last few weeks.

Shipments from England and France. Some had descriptions and insurance invoices, other didn't. Makes me think some of these crates weren't filled with paintings, especially if they weren't insured. No one transports art around the world without some kind of protection."

"Now you're thinking like a cop. Print all the lists and thanks." Conlon patted him on the shoulder and left.

Stone sat in his cramped hotel room pondering his next move. Finally, he picked up the phone and called Gamble. "I don't have anything concrete to tell you. The men in front of the building look familiar, but I don't know their identities or who they work for."

"It was worth a shot," replied Gamble. "Call me if you come up with anything else." He hung up the phone, disturbed by the conversation. It was only a feeling, but he knew Stone was lying.

"Jen, I've got some news. When can we meet?"

"I'm about ready to flee this place. Why don't you come to my place about six-thirty."

Conlon checked his watch. It was six o'clock. "Sounds good. Oh, and call Gamble." As he moved through the rush-hour traffic, he contemplated using his siren, but opted instead for the back alleys and managed to bluff someone out of the last parking space on the block. Jennifer unlocked the back entrance as both he and Gamble entered the alley behind her building.

"What's all this about?" she asked, once inside.

"First, we've got some prints off the parking stub. Nothing on them yet, but should know soon." Conlon pulled a list from his inside jacket pocket that explained Etting's discoveries. "Even though you haven't been charged with anything, I'm mincemeat if the DA finds out I gave you this." He opened it on the table so they all could see and began explaining. When he finished, he sat back and waited for questions.

"You think that young girl was killed because she found out what was going on?"

"Maybe, or she may have tried a little blackmail. I don't think she had a clue who she was dealing with."

"Let me look at that list." Gamble reached for the paper. "I recognize four names from the museum board." He leaned back in his chair and let out a deep sigh. "It's very disconcerting to know that people who purport to support the arts buy stolen paintings. At my age, nothing should surprise me, but it does. Then again, maybe they weren't aware of what they were doing."

"Which ones are we going to visit?"

He looked at the list again and placed a check next to four names.

Jennifer smiled. "All women? All these years, you've kept this side of you hidden from me."

"Must be my fatal charm," he said mockingly. "It should be easy enough to arrange the appointments. Getting information may be more difficult. No one likes to be confronted with the fact that they were duped into consorting with the black market, at great expense, I might add. Add the possibility that they may have to return the artwork translates into total embarrassment, something the rich don't tolerate lightly."

"How can they possibly expect to keep them?"

"How do we find the real owners and how could they claim ownership?"

"I don't know, there must be ways to prove it."

"Even if someone came forward, they would have

to prove it by producing sales agreements or pictures or insurance policies, most of which were destroyed or lost during the war. The Nazis may have been sticklers for detail, but for obvious reasons didn't leave much of a paper trail in this instance. You have to understand, this is a problem that experts have been struggling with for years."

"Then, why are we chasing after all this?" she asked.

"Sometimes, the rightful owner is found. We have Stone's promise to cooperate, but he needs to convince the authorities he's telling the truth. The more evidence he has, the better."

"You're right, but it's so frustrating."

"Let me have that list." Gamble handed it to Conlon. "That way I can keep tabs on you two and if one of these people decides to call my chief and chew his head off, I've got to have some ammo to calm him down." He looked at the four checked names. "Is there anything special I need to know about any of these, other than the fact that they're all very rich and have all kinds of political clout?"

"Isn't that enough?" asked Gamble. "Now, if you'll excuse me, I'll use the phone in your study and see what can be done."

"He won't admit it," said Jennifer, once he was out of earshot, "but this is taking a heavy toll on him. He and Marko are having the time of their lives, but all this running around is too much for them."

"Don't look at me to say anything. He's all yours."

Later that evening, Conlon dropped Gamble off at his place and went back to the station. Atkins and Klein were waiting. The overtime was racking up.

"We're not getting anywhere with the wool fibers. They're too common," said Atkins. "If we're lucky to stumble on the jacket, then the lab says it can do a match, but there's no way we can narrow it down as to who sold it. Every decent department store carries them."

"Run the prints on the parking stubs through the FBI and the Army. I've got a hunch."

Chapter Thirteen

The next morning, with Jennifer behind the wheel, she and Gamble began their search for the paintings mentioned on the list. Their first stop took them to Milton, a tony suburb south of the city. Taking the expressway out of town, they turned off at the East Milton exit and continued to Milton Hill where several old mansions that once belonged to sea captains and ship owners during the eighteenth and nineteenth centuries still maintained their colonial splendor.

Gamble directed her to a large white structure, beautifully landscaped, complete with a widow's walk, where the wives of sea captains once watched, with anxious hearts, hoping for their husbands' return from journeys that sometimes lasted more than three years.

A maid showed them into the solarium. The morning sun warmed the room as it filtered through the glass roof and the sweet smells of several different flowering plants permeated the air. Lilly Hamilton sat at an antique hand-carved mahogany desk, busily answering her correspondence. She was nearly seventy, at least that's what Jennifer had been led to believe, but she looked barely fifty. A tall woman with a slender frame, she rose from her desk with style and grace, the product of an excellent finishing school. Her hair, streaked with blond, was pulled gently from an angular well-formed face. The thought of a few facelifts flashed through Jennifer's mind. Gold hoops dangled from her ears. Dressed in gray silk pants and matching oversized shirt, she looked every bit the hostess she was. A dowager of the Boston social scene, Jennifer's acquaintance with her dated back several years.

"You haven't been to see me for quite a while, Gamble," she opened with a twinkle in her eye, "but I won't scold you. I'm sure you've been quite busy." She extended a lingering kiss on his cheek and turned to Jennifer. "And you, my dear, grow more beautiful each time I see you." Taking both their arms, she led them to a small seating area in front of a bank of floor-to-ceiling windows, overlooking a large well-manicured garden. She poured coffee from a large silver service, one that could have graced any museum of note. "You sounded so mysterious on the phone."

"I apologize, Lilly, but the subject is of a delicate nature and I wanted to discuss it with you in person."

"This gets more intriguing by the moment." She handed them each a bone china cup and saucer, then settled back in her chair, carefully balancing her own saucer on her knee.

Gamble began. "Several years ago you purchased two paintings from a company calling itself Art International."

"I've acquired several pieces from them. Why?"

"I'm particularly interested in a small Impressionist painting purchased in July of 1964."

"It's one of my favorites. Come, I'll show you." She led them into the front hall past a series of ancestral portraits and up to the first-floor landing of the main staircase. "Isn't it lovely?"

Gamble moved closer to examine it. Then he pulled an old photograph from his jacket pocket and held it next to the painting. It was the same. "Do you remember who sold it to you?"

"Why, yes. It was a lovely English gentleman. He was quite tall, good-looking, somewhere in his forties. Why are you asking me these questions?"

"Let's go back and sit down. We've got a lot to talk about and I doubt you're going to like it."

For the next fifteen minutes, they told her of their discoveries and suspicions. As they anticipated, the news was not to her liking. Gamble pulled out two photographs of Stone and handed her one. "Do you recognize this man? Picture him younger without the gray hair."

"He could be the one who sold me the painting, but it's hard to tell."

He showed her the second one, taken in Paris in 1948. "What about this one?"

"That's him. I'm sure. He later sold me two others, but I subsequently sold them."

Gamble smiled and put the pictures back in his pocket. "You may have to tell all this to the police, but not now."

"I must caution you not to tell anyone about this meeting. It could be dangerous," said Jennifer. "Promise me."

"If you say so, of course. Now what happens? What about my painting?"

"For now, nothing, you may even be able to keep it, but I can't promise anything." They stood up to go.

"You've been a big help, Lilly. We'll let ourselves out."

"Don't stay away so long, Gamble," she called as they retreated toward the front door.

"I'm getting a whole new picture of you," said Jennifer as they headed down the hall. "You're like a sailor with a girl in every port, only you've got them all in one place, Boston. Or am I not seeing the whole picture?"

"I've always enjoyed the company of beautiful and intelligent women. At my age, an evening of good company and conversation keeps me young. A little harmless flirting is a bonus. I've led a full life."

"Full. It's overflowing and the tap's still running." She laughed. "Where to now?" she asked as they fastened their seat belts.

"Not far, to Brush Hill Road." He gave her the directions as she drove down the short brick drive to the street.

Ten minutes later, they entered the plush grounds of an estate under the arch of a stone gatehouse fronting the street. Tiver House, a huge white wooden structure, lay hidden a quarter of a mile from the public eye. They parked in front and rang the bell. A maid ushered them out to a terrace that overlooked a large English garden. Lee and Nancy Heatherton, the owners, were reading the morning paper, enjoying a late breakfast. No introductions were necessary, for the four had known each other socially for years.

"Can I interest you in bacon and eggs?"

"No thanks, Lee, but coffee would be nice."

"What brings you to the country?" asked their hostess as she poured.

Gamble proceeded to outline a limited version of their tale, giving them what facts they needed to know.

"We bought several paintings from that company. Which ones are you interested in?"

Gamble took out his list and photos, placing them on the table. Nancy picked up one of the pictures and held it up for a better view. "This one's in the dining room. I can't believe we were so stupid. I knew the price was too good to be true."

"It's not your fault. You thought you were dealing with a legitimate art dealer," said Jennifer. "In fact, some of the pieces you purchased most likely are perfectly above board."

"He came highly recommended and seemed so nice."

"Who sent you to him?"

"Tom McIntyre. He's on every board in the city. He said he met him in a London gallery. You don't think he could be mixed up in all of this?"

"I doubt it. What did this man look like, the one who sold you the painting?"

"He was English, tall, acted as though he might be ex-military. Does that help?" asked Lee.

Jennifer nodded. "Yes. This could get nasty. Please don't mention this meeting to anyone. These people are dangerous. They've already committed two murders."

Nancy grabbed her husband's arm. "That killing in the art gallery. I never thought about it. We've been there. Dear heaven."

"If I need any more information, I'll contact you. Meanwhile, relax. You're not in danger," said Gamble.

"What about the police?"

"We're working with them," said Jennifer. "If you have any suspicion that you're in any danger, call the local police and ask them to get in touch with Lieutenant Conlon in the city."

"I'd like to take the painting with me," said Gamble. "I'll make sure it's properly taken care of."

"Of course, if it will help. How could we have been such fools?" Lee wrapped the painting and walked the two of them to the car. In the rear-view mirror, Jennifer could see him watching as they drove away.

"I think we frightened them," she said. "I hope they don't panic."

"Lee's got a good head on his shoulders. I wouldn't worry."

"Why did you want the painting?"

"To run some tests."

"Tests? Why?"

"I'm not sure yet, but if I'm right, we've stumbled on a very lucrative swindle."

"You think it's a forgery, too."

"It's almost a certainty."

"Looks like we have a pretty good case for that, but it doesn't get us any closer to our murderer." She slowed for a red light. "Where to?"

"Now we go to Wellesley and Newton, but first, I need sustenance. There's a restaurant at the junction of Route 138 and the Interstate. Let's stop there."

An hour later, they were back on the road heading north. The results were the same as the morning. The paintings were examined and the problem discussed. Each owner promised to say nothing of the visit and to cooperate with the police when the time came.

"You have a strange look on your face," commented Jennifer as they drove back to the city. "What did you see that I missed?"

"I'm not sure, but I want your father's input, a different perspective. My suspicious nature has been piqued. One more thing, we're being followed."

"I'm glad you waited until now to tell me. This cloak-and-dagger stuff makes me nervous. My phone's in the console. Call Dad and tell him we're on our way."

Brand McCallum pushed the plaid woolen blanket from his lap and, bracing himself on the iron railing, cautiously pulled himself to a bent-over standing position. Sweat poured from his forehead and his hands trembled as he squeezed the black metal for dear life. His lungs burned as he gasped for air. He steadied himself and stood erect. For days he had been pushing himself, enduring excruciating pain and now, finally, he could stand.

He counted to sixty and slowly sank back into the chair. It seemed like such a small achievement for a man who had done so much with his life, but today, it was the highlight of his accomplishments. Such a shame he couldn't share it with anyone. The doctors had forbidden any kind of strenuous exercise for at least another week.

He pulled the blanket about his knees and sat back, trying to catch his breath. He was content. Years of patience conditioned him to taking one thing at a time. Reaching for a glass of water, he drank slowly, thankful that at age seventy-nine, he was still alive. The last few months had forced him to contemplate the finality of life and instilled a determination to enjoy his friends and children for as long as possible. He wanted to walk his daughter down the aisle, if only she'd make up her mind.

For days, he had been reminiscing, looking back on his life, remembering the good and the bad. Every day, his beautiful wife Sybil dominated his thoughts. She slipped through his dreams as he sat dozing in the afternoon sun, always bringing a smile to his face.

When they met in 1946, she was a twenty-one-year-old senior at Wellesley, the exceptionally beautiful

daughter of a United States Senator. They married in
1948 and immediately moved to Washington where he
continued his post as one of the many special advisors
to the President and a relationship with the newly
formed CIA. Then several years as a professor at Har-
vard Law and an appointment to the Federal District
Court followed. His ties to the intelligence community
remained firm and he often acted as a consultant on
top-secret matters.

His two children were his pride and joy. William,
now in the Foreign Service and attached to The Hague,
was a competent well-rounded diplomat. William was
married to a lovely woman, with two small children,
and Brand missed them more than he could express.
And Jennifer, how he loved her; the joy of his life, so
much like Sybil. So much her own person, bright, interesting and full of life.

Now she was involved in a complicated and difficult
situation with his oldest and dearest friend and it worried him. In fact, it had dominated his thoughts for the
last several days. Gamble's phone call had come at a
perfect time.

Suddenly, footsteps in the hall jolted him back to
the present. His company had arrived.

With the amenities over, the three began thrashing
out the subject at hand. "Did you give any thought to
the idea of forgeries?" asked Brand.

"You must have been reading my mind," replied his
old friend.

"Why would these people sell the originals when
they could make copies and palm them off to unsuspecting individuals as the real thing? They could sell
the same subject three or four times and no one would
be the wiser."

"What if two people who owned the same painting
came in contact with each other?" asked Jennifer.

"In the unlikely event that that happened, each would assume the other had the forgery and they'd go home feeling smug and happy that they owned the real one. Besides, who could they complain to? No one likes to be made a fool of. Better to suffer silently than have others find out. The rich are quite vain."

"I think you're on the right track," offered Brand.

"You mean to tell me that nice couple paid a small fortune for a copy?"

"I'm not completely sure yet, but yes, it happens every day."

"But Nancy thought she was dealing with a legitimate dealer. We could get Stone for grand theft," said Jennifer.

"Among other things, but right now we have to solve two murders and I think I know how."

"We're going about this the wrong way. We're going backwards. We need to go forward," said Brand.

"And how are we supposed to do that?" she asked.

"All we've got are the paintings. We'll start with them. What does your schedule look like for the next few days?"

"Busy, but I can rearrange things, why?"

"You and Gamble and Marko are going to Paris and from there, heaven knows."

"Paris! I'm not sure about this."

"He's right," said Gamble. "We have to follow their trail and that begins with the theft. I've got a few leads from Stone, but most of it we'll have to ferret out on our own. We need evidence."

Jennifer could see his face come alive. His brain was working in overdrive. Even her father's expression had changed. The two were back at work, doing the thing they did best; following the trail, putting clues together and making a case. She saw a wistful look in her father's eyes. He wanted in on the action, but knew it was impossible. How she wished she had known them back then. It must have been wonderful.

She stopped daydreaming and returned to the conversation. "I don't have any court appearances scheduled for two weeks and my assistants can handle things for a while. You'll have to give me a couple of days, though. I can't just pack my bags and disappear. How long will we be gone?"

"Four or five days at the most."

I assume we can't tell anyone where we're going."

"What are you going to tell Conlon?" asked her father.

"I'll call him from the airport twenty minutes before takeoff and leave a message on his machine. Right away, he'll know something's up, but it will be too late. Then he'll call you. Tell him the truth. He'll hit the ceiling, but you can take it."

"You are the devious one." Her father smiled.

"Must run in the family."

Chapter Fourteen

It was a little after nine P.M. when the cab dropped Jennifer at Terminal C for the eleven o'clock Air France flight from Logan Airport to Paris. Checking her bags curbside, she bypassed the long lines at the ticket counter, passed through security check, and headed for the restaurant located opposite their gate. She found her traveling companions, Gamble and Marko Bertoni, watching the planes. Dregs of fried clams and French fries lay evident on their plates.

"We're going to be fed in lavish style on the plane. Why on earth are you eating?"

"It's that or the bar. I suggested we get into the Parisian mode with a good bottle of cabernet, but your mentor declined. He said we had to wait for you," said Marko.

"Too much alcohol is not a good thing when flying. It enhances jet lag."

"Precisely what I said," offered Gamble with a straight face. "Have you checked in?"

"No, I'll do that when the gate opens. You two are incorrigible." Wearily, she sank into one of the available hard metal chairs and tried to catch the waitress's attention. "I hope you have some kind of a plan."

"You wound me to the quick, young lady. Of course, we have a plan, don't we Marko?"

"Most assuredly. I've arranged for someone to meet us at Charles DeGaulle. From there, they'll take us to Paris and fill us in on their latest information. Then, we go to Marseilles and then to Avignon. Hopefully, we'll be able to follow the exact trail the paintings took so many years ago. Then, perhaps we'll find out who's using the route now."

"Sounds like a wild goose chase to me. All that happened fifty years ago."

Gamble continued. "The system was planned for the long haul. It wasn't a one-time thing. A variety of contraband is moving through the very same channels today. We need to find it."

Jennifer eyed the gate attendant opening up her station and looked at her watch. "I'm going to check in and make a few calls. I forgot to leave some last-minute instructions on my office voice mail. Then, I'll call Conlon. Thank heaven, he's working tonight. He won't check his machine until after midnight and we'll be gone. I'll meet you at the gate."

She handed Gamble her carry-on. "Hold this for me. I don't want someone walking off with it." She left in search for an available phone and the gift shop to buy a couple of magazines. Thirty minutes later, they were strapping themselves into comfortable roomy leather business class seats. The flight attendant offered champagne, but she opted for a bottle of water. A little wine at dinner would be enough to lull her to sleep during the six-hour flight.

They arrived in Paris early the next morning. Donat Pental, the grandson of an old Resistance colleague, met them with a sign bearing Marko's name. Pleasantries expressed, the weary travelers were chauffeured to a spacious well-maintained home on the outskirts of the capital. As they passed through the countryside, the two men talked of years past, resurrecting memories, both sad and pleasant.

On their arrival, their host, Jacques Pental greeted his old friend and his companions with genuine warmth and enthusiasm. "It has been many years, my old friend." He gave Marko a fierce hug and stood back to examine the man before him. "A little older, perhaps, but the same."

"And you. The years have been kind."

"I can't complain." He extended a hand to Gamble. "It is good to meet you, Monsieur. And this must be Jennifer." He embraced her, kissing her on both cheeks. "I owe your father my life. I'll do whatever I can to help. Now, you must be tired." He turned to an attractive woman about fifty standing by the door. "This is my daughter, Claudine. She'll show you to your rooms. Rest for a few hours and we'll talk later. By then, I should have more news."

At seven-thirty, they reconvened over dinner. Jacques introduced his guest to the rest of his large family, postponing the important discussion until dessert.

"Now, I am sure you are anxious to hear what information we have gathered. Emil, bring the map." The young man left the room and reappeared a moment later with two maps, one of France and one of

Paris. Jennifer helped clear the table as Jacques spread them flat so they all could see.

"Let me begin here," he said as he pinpointed a section of the city. "We know that the paintings were taken from the museum here and transported to Marseilles and left at a warehouse near the waterfront. It took them nearly three days, for the roads were in very bad condition. The drivers returned by train, well paid for their services. The Allies watched the ports and the roads, but instead of transporting them out of the country, they kept them hidden for more than three months. From there, they were moved to an ancient chateau on the outskirts of Avignon."

"How do you know all this?" asked Jennifer.

"The Resistance was still active after the war and always in need of money. The Free French and the Communists, along with countless political factions were vying for power. Sometimes, it was necessary to do things we were not proud of. No one in my small group was responsible, but another small band aided in the robbery. We are sure an Englishman was in charge and suspect it is your Major Stone. The description fits. He calls himself Livingstone now and still lives in the chateau."

"Go on," said Gamble. "This agrees with what Stone told me."

"You have seen him?"

"He came to see me in Boston. He's frightened."

"Men in trouble often do unpredictable things." He pulled out the map of France and drew a circle around the Marseilles area. "The Englishman purchased the old chateau in Avignon shortly after the war and spent many months remodeling it. No local artisans or laborers were used. Everything was done in secret. You can imagine what the villagers thought of that. Now, he has a good rapport with them. He buys all his food and supplies from the surrounding farms and shops in the town. He lends money at no interest to those in need. And he has built them a new school and repaired their church. They have come to idolize him. If there is trouble, they will be on his side."

"What you're saying is we're on our own."

Jacques nodded. "There were rumors that a special room with some kind of modern heating and cooling was installed in the old barn. Perhaps your paintings are there."

"What about the paintings themselves?"

"Nothing happened for nearly two years. Then slowly a few pictures began to surface. They were not great finds or famous works, but they were good, most dating around the turn of the century. Impressionists were becoming fashionable. My experts here in Paris knew of the collection and though no one ever knew what it contained, there was much speculation. Some were sold to museums, some to private collections, even an occasional auction. What with all the problems, no one questioned their ownership. You realize much of this information comes from those engaged in illegal activities. The police may not accept its veracity."

Conlon nodded. "I knew about the sales, but the rest is new. I believe some of them are forgeries sold to unsuspecting, but greedy people."

"I am getting to that. Some say there is a studio on the second floor of the barn where artists are busy at work, doing as you suspect. There has been more than one disgruntled patron of the arts, unable to go to the police, who have voiced their anger. Somehow, they have been mollified. I suppose their money was returned, hoping to avoid embarrassment, but in the art world, there are no secrets. People love to talk."

"Can we get into this studio?"

"There is tight security, but no system is burglar-proof, we proved that on more than one occasion, have we not?"

"That was many years ago," said Marko. "It may be too difficult for us now."

Ah," replied Jacques, "but not for my grandsons. I run a security company now. You would be surprised how many celebrities and politicians need protection for their property and themselves. It has become quite a lucrative business. Occasionally, we test the systems of our clients. It keeps my employees on their toes and gives them a little excitement. Like us, they look for the thrill."

He turned to his grandsons. "They are the best and are ready to go with you. One of my clients was a victim of Stone's swindle. I feel it is my duty to help."

"I can't let you get mixed up in this. Information is one thing, but to expose you to arrest or even death. No. No," exclaimed Marko.

"I am not about to let you have all the fun. I may not be able to go with you, but I will be there in spirit. Tomorrow, you will take the train to Marseilles and Donet will go with you. From there, a cousin will take you to the warehouse. They are still using it. Then to Avignon. A friend of the family has offered his home. It is quite near your target and he has decided to visit his daughter in Lyon. You will have complete privacy to organize your plan of action."

Gamble stood up, grimacing as his bones creaked. "Looks as though we have a long day ahead of us. I believe it is time to retire."

"Me, too," said Marko. "My aching body is reminding me of my age." The two men left in deep conversation, obviously looking forward to their new adventure.

Jennifer remained behind. "Monsieur Pental, what

did you mean when you said my father saved your life?"

"In 1943, your father was smuggled by boat to Calais and taken by an underground route to Paris to meet with Resistance members. Somehow, the Germans discovered he was here. When they raided the meeting, I was shot. Your father carried me to safety and I spent many weeks recuperating. This is the result of my injury." He tapped his cane against an artificial leg. "Your father stayed to finish his mission and we smuggled him back to England. We believe we were betrayed by one of our own."

"He never talked about his work. It's just been lately that I've learned anything at all about his exploits."

"Most of his accomplishments will never be revealed. Your father is a great patriot and a fine man. I can never repay him."

"Gamble didn't mention it, but he's in a great deal of trouble. If we can bring back proof that this network is still in existence, it may help clear him of a possible murder charge." She stood up to leave. "And now, if I don't get some sleep, I'll be of no use tomorrow. The jet lag has finally hit me." She leaned over and planted a tiny kiss on her host's cheek. "Good night and thank you." Once upstairs, she undressed and fell asleep seconds after her head hit the pillow.

Early the next morning, Gamble, Marko, and Jennifer, accompanied by Donet and his brother, Victor, boarded the TGV, the fastest train on earth, for the two-hour trip to Marseilles. Emil, a cousin of the Pentals, met them at the station and drove them by the warehouse, parking a few doors away.

"It looks deserted," said Jennifer.

"As of yesterday, they were still in business. A man has been watching it since Marko's phone call. There is a lot of activity, mostly deliveries, but very few orders leaving the building."

"Looks as though they're stocking up, but with what?"

"I could hazard a good guess," said Gamble.

"Guns. Harrington's probably waiting for the right moment to ship them out," offered Marko.

"Any chance we could get a look inside?" asked Gamble.

"Maybe. It will be difficult, Monsieur. They have a good alarm system and dogs, but perhaps we could slip in tonight and look around." Emil checked his watch. "But first, you need to register at the hotel."

He drove them to a small, quiet, privately owned inn not far from the city. "It belongs to my family. We may speak freely here." He helped with the baggage and arranged for their check-in. "I would like you to meet my friends. They are waiting for us in the dining room. They have agreed to help."

He guided them through a set of French doors to a small cozy room containing six tables set up for the noon meal. Two men sat at a round table in the corner by a large window. "Names are not important, I hope you understand."

"Emil has told us of your problem," began the oldest. "How may we be of help?" Dressed as laborers in nondescript baggy pants and bland shirts, they hardly looked the part of accomplished operatives.

"I need to know what's in that warehouse. I understand it may be a problem."

"The security system is good, but my friends can bypass it. There are no guards, but the dogs are let loose every night. They may be trained not to eat anything that is not given to them by their trainer, so we will use, how do you say, a spray that will put them to sleep. We should be in and out in half an hour. May I suggest you allow us to do the actual work?"

"Agreed, but I would like to wait in the car."

"That can be arranged. We go tonight."

Gamble waited in a black van and watched as the four young men bypassed the alarm system and slipped into the rear entrance of the building. He heard dogs barking and then total silence. In less than twenty minutes, they returned. Emil slipped behind the wheel as the others climbed into the back seat. They drove away slowly into the dark.

"There are at least fifty large wooden crates filled with semi-automatics and ammunition. There is also another small room that is air-conditioned. At first, I thought it was an office, but there is no window. I found two small crates sealed and marked fragile, ready for shipment. They might be your paintings." He handed Gamble a piece of paper. "I copied the address on the front of them."

Gamble turned on the overhead light. It was the Newbury Street address of the gallery. He slipped the paper into his pocket and smiled.

"Tomorrow, we go to Avignon?"

"Yes, tomorrow we go."

The Frenchmen and three Americans set off for Avignon the next day. They arrived before noon, going directly to the rented cottage. The owner was gone, but Gamble found the key on a hook hanging by the back door. "Trusting souls," he said as he unlocked the door and they stepped inside.

It was a comfortable room with a large fireplace filling the back wall. Brightly colored slipcovers expressed a casual country look. Sturdy oak furniture, fresh flowers, crisp white curtains and several pillows, casually placed on the comfortable couches, completed the effect. Each claimed a bedroom and met back in the kitchen.

Emil found a note taped to the refrigerator. "The housekeeper has left the noon meal for us and will return to prepare dinner." He checked the large cauldron on the stove. "Veal stew," he offered. Jennifer helped him with the preparations as they discussed their next move.

"The chateau is about a mile from here," continued Emil as he ladled soup in large earthen bowls and set them on the huge battered pine table. "When the owner is there, he has a staff of five, but only the housekeeper and gardener, the Garons remain. They are married and live in an apartment in the kitchen wing. On Tuesday, that is tomorrow, they go to the village and shop. We will go then."

He joined the rest of them at the table. "There is also a large barn, but no one is allowed inside. Also, three men come and stay several weeks at a time and then leave. They frequent the only café in town. They could be your forgers."

"Where are they now?" asked Jennifer.

"They have not been seen in the village for more than two weeks."

"Then, Tuesday it is," said Marko. "Meanwhile, relax. Emil, you and I are going to drive by the chateau and then to the town hall to look up the deed. Let's see who holds title to the property." Grabbing his coat, he headed for the door. "Enjoy the incredible French countryside from the patio."

Emil drove while Marko gathered his thoughts. "Does this Englishman have a business in town?"

"No, he has led everyone to believe that his wealth is from the family. The people here respect that. Old money represents power to them. He is well liked now and spends his money freely with the merchants, unlike many newcomers who come here, restore our wonderful mansions, and ignore the village. We need their support to live, but they do not care."

Emil slowed as they passed the chateau, a property surrounded by a tall thick wall. The gate was closed. A keypad, attached to an iron post, stood to the left of the driveway. The house could be seen from the distance, large and imposing, outlined by a clear blue sky.

Emil pulled off to the side of the road. "The wall is electrified and there are security cameras at intervals around the perimeter." He pointed to a tree about twenty feet from the gate with a large limb extending over the wall. "But, they are careless. That limb should have been removed and there is no camera. They must think this area is covered by the one at the gate. We will climb the tree and use the branch to get over the wall."

"I've got to get in there, but not that way, I'll never make it."

"Once inside, I will let you in. The servants use a back entrance. There is a camera there also, but it can be temporarily disconnected. We do not want your face on film, now do we?" He chuckled. "Don't worry, Grandpapa trained us to be very careful. How much time do we need once we are inside?"

"About half an hour, enough time to look around and take some pictures."

"That will not be a problem."

The back road was deserted as Emil skirted the property and arrived at the back gate. "After we are in, drive here and wait for us. I will open the gate."

They moved on and arrived in the village in a matter of minutes. Emil disappeared to check out the town while Marko went directly to the town hall. The clerk

showed him the latest book containing property trans-
fers. He noted that some of the dates went back many
hundreds of years.

He looked up the property in question. It had belonged to one family for many years. The only transfer
recorded was in 1949. He copied the information and
went in search of his driver. He found him sitting at
a sidewalk table in the town's only café. They enjoyed
an afternoon coffee and returned to the villa.

They left the next day. The men tried and failed to
persuade Jennifer to stay behind. A few minutes later,
they pulled up to the chateau entrance. Emil and his
brother jumped from the rear of the van and scurried
up the tree. With Jennifer and Marko in the back seat,
Gamble drove to the back gate and turned off the ig-
nition. Ten minutes later, Emil unlocked the iron post
and let them in. He led them up a narrow dirt drive
to a large stone barn several hundred feet behind the
chateau. "My brother is checking the main house, but
I think what you are looking for will be in here." He
opened the door and stepped inside first.

"There are no cameras or sensors, but be careful
what you touch. I wasn't able to check everything."

Jennifer climbed the stairs to the second floor and
opened each door as she made her way to the end of
the building. Halfway down the hall she found what
they were looking for. "In here," she called and
stepped into a huge room filled with light from the
several skylights placed in the ceiling.

The room smelled of paint and turpentine. Three
paint boxes, closed and fastened tightly, sat on separate tables with an empty easel placed beside each one.
Rolls of canvas lay on the floor. Several pieces, already sized and stretched, rested against a wall. Above
them, a number of completed paintings hung on the

wall. She was about to take a closer look when Gamble came through the door and stopped in his tracks.

"My God!" he exclaimed. "They've got regular assembly line going here." He walked slowly along the wall, gently touching a few of the paintings. "They're still wet." He carefully removed one from the wall, scrutinizing it with a practiced eye. "They're good, quite good, almost perfect. The colors are right and the pigment looks authentic. With a little aging, they could fool a lot of people."

He placed the painting back on the wall and stepped back to glimpse all of them. "Amazing." He removed the camera from around his neck and, using a wide-angle lens, began snapping. Changing lenses, he concentrated on each painting, taking shots from every angle, carefully taking close-ups of every frame.

"I found a gallery at the end of the hall," said Marko as he poked his head through the door. "There must be hundreds of paintings covering the walls." He let out a deep gasp when he finally noticed the back wall. "Are they what I think they are?"

"Correct the first time." Gamble hung the camera back around his neck. "Let's take a look at what you've found. We haven't much time, but I can't leave without pictures."

Jennifer joined him as he followed Marko down the hall into an immense area with a high ceiling and an elaborate panel of switches, obviously the controls for a complicated lighting arrangement. The air was cool and dry, climate controlled to ensure the paintings' integrity.

"All the bells and whistles," said Jennifer as she moved inside. "This must be the showroom, a dog-and-pony show for prospective buyers. I've go to hand it to our Mr. Stone. He knows how to merchandise.

The buyers are shown the real thing, then go home with a fake."

Gamble resumed taking pictures, moving as fast as he could. He was nearly finished when Emil rushed into the room.

"We must leave. We've already stayed too long."

They ran down the drive to their waiting car. Emil gunned the engine as they sped down the dirt road.

"Now, what do we do? All this is inadmissible in a court of law. Breaking and entering is still considered a felony, even in France," said Jennifer as Emil drove them to the Marseilles train station the next morning.

"If my plan works, there won't be a trial," said Gamble.

"Well, are you planning on telling me what that is?"

"First, I get the pictures developed. They should all come out, unless I've lost my touch. Then, I confront Stone. There's nothing preventing me from sharing them with the French authorities. He doesn't want to spend the last few years of his life in prison. Then, there's the Army. Technically, he's AWOL. He needs us to put in a good word for him. H's already offered to help and he's terrified. He'll testify."

"He may be more afraid of Timmy Harrington than he is of the law."

Chapter Fifteen

They arrived at Logan Airport the next afternoon and breezed through customs. As they emerged into the main terminal area, two uniformed officers and a couple of detectives suddenly surrounded them.

"Gamble Coulhoon, you're under arrest for the murders of René DeLacroix and Elena Lassiter." The detective read him his rights and handcuffed him.

Jennifer recognized Atkins and Klein. "What's going on?"

"The DA found out he left the country and is afraid he'll skip out of his jurisdiction again. He's looking for a fast arraignment and is asking for no bail."

"That's garbage. He's after me, Gamble. I'm sorry. You'll have to go with them. Give me the pictures. I'll have them developed and maybe, if I show them to that fool, he'll back off."

Gamble produced the film. "I'm confident everything will work out. Call your father, just to be on the safe side."

Jennifer watched as they led him away to the waiting squad car. Then she left the terminal, barely controlling her anger as Marko approached the dispatcher to hail them a cab. She fumed as they rode through the tunnel. "There are moments when I could throttle that man. What burns me up the most is his method. He doesn't come for me—no, he tries to get to me through my clients and friends. He's playing dirty pool."

"Politics is never fair. You know that. It's got nothing to do with the law. What do you suggest we do next?"

"First, we drop off these pictures, then we go see Dad. Together you may be able to concoct a plan while I work on an alternative. Then, I swallow my pride and go see Conlon. Maybe he can tell me what's going on."

She asked the driver to stop at a one-hour photo place on Charles Street, then directed the cab to Louisburg Square. Marko paid the driver and they went inside. They found her father in the study, quietly reading.

"Gamble's been arrested."

"I know. Conlon called and told me about the DA's plans. He tried to prevent it, but his hands are tied, too much politics."

"So Marko keeps reminding me. Why am I constantly surprised when someone plays a dirty trick on me? I can't be that naive."

"Jennifer, you expect everyone to play fair and the game simply isn't played that way. You've got to learn to expect the worse, but give the best."

"I suppose. Now, what do we do?"

"First. Go help Gamble. I doubt he'll be detained

long. I think Mancuso is trying to throw a scare into him. There's not enough evidence to hold him. It's all show. Marko and I will put our heads together while you're at the police station."

Jennifer left them conspiring and walked down Beacon Hill. She desperately wanted to go home to shower and change, but went to the police station instead. After she identified herself as Gamble's attorney, the desk sergeant pointed her toward one of the interrogation rooms.

"Sorry I took so long." She noticed that he seemed tired and haggard, looking every bit his seventy-eight years. "Are you O.K.?"

"As well as can be expected."

"Have you spoken to anyone?"

"No, I told them I would wait for my attorney. Actually, the detectives didn't seem very enthusiastic about their job."

"They know the whole thing is bogus. At least we've got them on our side. Have you seen Conlon?"

"No, but he's in the building."

"I'll try to ambush him in his office. Maybe a surprise visit will put him off guard. I'm not in the mood to be chastised."

She found him on the phone, shaking his head with a frown spread across his face. She stood in the doorway and waited. When he looked up, the frown didn't disappear. Taking a seat, she waited for the lecture. Instead, he hung up the phone, settled back in his chair, and waited.

"Okay, so I should have told you we were leaving the country. I'm sorry."

"Do you have any idea what kind of furor you and your friends caused by this little jaunt? Sometimes, I wonder about you, I really do."

"If I told you we were going, you would have hit the ceiling."

"You're right about that. Do you know how worried I was? You could have been killed!"

"Well, we weren't. See." She stood up and turned around. "All in one piece."

"Stop clowning around. We've got a problem. Gamble's downstairs. The DA's out for blood."

"I know, but I think I have a way to calm him down." She told him of Gamble's plan and sat back, waiting. "What do you think?"

"Actually, it's not half bad. I don't know how the DA's going to react, but go ahead, ask. You don't have anything to lose."

"That's not exactly a vote of confidence, but I'll take it as a yes. What about Gamble?"

"We'll keep him for awhile, then he can leave. I'll have to put a tail on him to pacify Mancuso and to keep an eye on him. He could be in danger."

"Tell him, otherwise, he'll lose them. Your best are no match for him."

"You drive a hard bargain, counselor. Keep me up to speed, please. You may need the services of Boston's finest in a hurry."

"Agreed." She leaned across the desk and planted an affectionate kiss on his forehead. "I missed you. Now, I've got to tend to my client, but I'll be back."

"Try and stay out of trouble," he called as she headed back down the hall to the interrogation area.

She found Gamble deep in conversation with Atkins and Klein. "Hi guys. I hope you aren't infringing on my client's rights." They chuckled as she flashed a smile and joined them at the table. "Conlon says we have to kill some time, then we can go." She looked at Klein. "I guess than means you have to stay here with us."

"Sometimes I think the DA's gone over the edge. He's got that little worm, Romano snooping around." Klein walked over to the two-way mirror and pulled the blind. "I already turned off the microphone leading to the other room. I told him it was broken. It will drive the little rat crazy. He won't be able to complain 'cause he's not supposed to be poking his nose into ongoing investigations unless he's invited. I wonder what kind of a story he's going to dream up to keep Mancuso from jumping all over him."

"You don't like him, do you?" said Jennifer.

"What's there to like?" Atkins checked his watch. "I think we've wasted enough time. Sorry about this, Mr. Coulhoon."

"I want you to go to Dad's and wait," she said once they were outside. "I'm going to pick up the pictures and pay a visit to the District Attorney. If I'm successful, we can put your plan in motion."

"Wouldn't it be better if I went with you?"

She waved down a cab and opened the door. "That would be like waving a red flag in front of him. Sometimes, I think he's jealous of you. Deep inside he always wanted to be an international spy. He let that slip one night when we were working late. I'll call you when I leave his office. And one more thing, Conlon's going to put a tail on you. Don't try to lose them. It's for your protection and part of the deal. Besides, it will keep Mancuso quiet. Invite them in when you get to Dad's, I'm sure you'll all get along." She watched the cab drive away, then headed for the photo shop and the DA's office.

It was after five when she walked into Mancuso's outer office. His secretary was gone for the day, but the door to his inner sanctum was open. She could see her old boss, jacket off, tie loosened, sleeves rolled back, absorbed in the papers spread out on his desk. She knocked and waited for an invitation.

"Jennifer, what an interesting surprise. Come in." He removed his glasses and stretched his arms in the air. "It's been a long day, but then yours has been too. Pleasant flight?"

"You know, as I stood in the doorway, I was remembering the time we found the weak link in the Mitchell case. It was a nice thought. Don't spoil it."

"Sorry, I couldn't help it. Come in. Sit." He motioned to one of the large comfortable chairs in front of his desk. "I promise, no more jabs. You did a number on Romano. He's furious."

"Good." She looked around the room. "I see you've redecorated. New carpet, new draperies, even new artwork. A little modern for you, isn't it?"

"Change is a good thing. Initiates creativity."

"I'll get right to the point. What I'm going to say may help both of us. My client won't have to go to trial for a crime he didn't commit and you won't have to waste the taxpayers' money."

"I've got enough to indict."

"Everyone knows a good DA can get a Grand Jury to say yes to anything, making it stick is something else. Just listen."

"I'm all ears."

"Everything you have is circumstantial. The only witness to DeLacroix's argument with Gamble is dead. He freely admits he has a history with the stolen art, but if it weren't for him, you wouldn't know anything about it. No jury is going to believe that he would blow the whistle on a deal that he hoped to make millions on. The only other thing you have is his past association with the paintings.

"By the time I present, who knows how many character witnesses, including my father, the jury will vote for sainthood. Besides, the man is seventy-eight years old. Do you honestly think they will believe he murdered two people?

"You don't have any witnesses to either murder, but you have two people describing what sounds like the same man in the vicinity of both crime scenes and it's not Gamble. And you don't have the weapon. I know the pressure's on but don't jump the gun."

Mancuso sat back and waited while she cleared a space on his desk and replaced his papers with an envelope containing the pictures. As she talked, she watched his eyes. She knew that look. He was interested. She explained what they were doing in France. When she reached the part where they broke into the chateau, she began laying the photos out for him to see.

"What do you think?" She backed away from the desk, giving him room. He wasn't a man to be crowded.

"You actually broke into this place?"

"Don't start. I know it was wrong."

"Wrong! You could have been arrested."

"I've already had the lecture. I don't need to hear it again. Let me finish and then say your piece." She thought for a minute. Carefully chosen words were needed. "We've also got a tie-in with Timmy Harrington. How much do you want him?"

"As if you don't already know."

"Gamble wants to go to Stone—"

"If such a man exists."

"Oh, he exists. I've met him."

Mancuso shook his head but held his tongue. "Go on."

"Gamble will tell Stone that he's changed his mind and wants a piece of the action. That way the police won't get involved, he can get rich, and Stone can keep his operation."

"But the police are already involved."

"With the murders, yes, but not with forgery and embezzlement. They can continue their investigation and Stone will quietly disappear."

"I thought Stone wanted to come in."

"He does, only because he's afraid of Harrington. If Gamble suggests a way for it to all go away. . . ."

"And you think he'll go for it?"

"No, he'll panic and go to Harrington. He'll probably give him the smuggling route and might even throw in the paintings. He'll make Gamble the bad guy and hope to disappear and enjoy all that money in his Swiss bank accounts." She straightened up and returned to her chair. "When we arrest him, we'll make a deal in return for enough to convict Harrington."

"I don't like using civilians in police matters."

"He's not exactly new to the game. The man's had fifty years of experience at this sort of thing."

"You're sure he's not involved in this?"

"Why would we traipse all over France trying to find the paintings and then come back here if he's guilty?"

"You've got a point. I'm going to put a tail on him."

"Already taken care of. Conlon arranged it when Gamble left the police station. He's been notified and won't try to shake them."

"You've thought of just about anything. How can I say no? I don't want to make a fool of myself again and the Mayor would like to see this thing laid to rest." He tapped his pen on the desk and looked at the photo again. "All these paintings are hanging in a barn and the French authorities don't know it?"

"Think of the press coverage when you announce the discovery of a vast international stolen art ring, dating back to the war. You'll be a household word."

"Don't be facetious, young lady, although you do

have a point." He took a deep breath. "Go ahead and set it up. Make sure Conlon has Coulhoon covered round the clock. I don't want the old man's death on my conscience."

"Thanks. You won't regret it."

"How many times have I heard that before."

"I take back all those awful things I've said about you." She stood there for a moment, not quite sure of herself. "You and I, we used to have some good times."

"We could again. We may not always see eye to eye, but I think we respect each other. When this is over, come talk to me, I've got a proposition for you."

"Sounds interesting."

"It is."

Jennifer got up to leave.

"I want to be kept in the loop, every step. Do I make myself clear?"

"Deal."

Chapter Sixteen

Conlon, Gamble, and Jennifer met with the DA in his office the next morning. They went over the plan, exhausting every angle, plugging holes, trying to ensure nothing could go wrong.

"I'm not crazy about this idea," said Mancuso when they finished, "but Jennifer's convinced me it's the only way to get to the bottom of these murders."

"Not to mention a huge black-market art ring and the chance to get something on Timmy Harrington," added Gamble.

"Point noted. Set it up. I want this case gone as much as you do." Mancuso stood up and extended his hand to Gamble. "Over the years, I've heard a lot about you and never expected we would be part of the same operation. I hope this turns out well."

"I would hate to end my career on a negative note," replied Gamble.

Outside, the three stopped to make final arrangements.

"You had to stick it to him, didn't you?" said Jennifer to Gamble.

"Couldn't help myself. I thought he took it very well."

"Try and behave yourself," she pleaded.

Conlon returned to the station to put things in motion. Atkins and Klein were both at their desks. He called them into his office. "We've got a lot to discuss, so listen up."

Klein shut the door. "What's up?"

"I'm calling off the regular tail on Conlon. You two drop everything and stick to him like glue. Pick two others you can rely on. It means twelve-hour shifts, but this is top priority. The DA's approved a plan that's going to be dicey. That means, be on your toes."

"What if he tries to lose us? He's still pretty good."

"He won't. The whole thing is his idea."

"I like the old guy," said Atkins. "I hope this doesn't mean the DA's going to turn around and bag him for the murders."

"No, it means he's hanging himself out to dry to try and catch the killer."

"Are we after Harrington?"

"Coulhoon doesn't think so."

"Then who? It would be nice to know who we're supposed to be trying to catch."

"That's the problem. We don't know. Coulhoon's going to arrange a meeting with Stone. What happens after that is what we have to worry about."

"Is he wearing a wire?"

"No. Too dangerous. Stone's right on the edge and we're afraid he'll bolt if he suspects a trap."

"I don't like this," said Klein. "Too many things can go wrong."

"All we can do is wait for Gamble's signal."

"When do we start?"

"Now."

Gamble asked Jennifer to make a stop at the Museum of Art. They entered the building and walked back to the restoration area. There they met Sandra Anderson, a friend of Gamble's and one of the foremost experts on the Impressionist period. They found her in her workshop busily examining a painting in a serious state of decomposition. Gamble made the introductions.

"I wasn't sure you would be available."

"I assume you're referring to my brief encounter with the local police."

"All cleared up, I hope."

"I'm working on it," said Jennifer.

"Have you had a chance to examine the painting I left with you last week?"

"You were right. It's a fake. A good reproduction, but still a fake." She went to the back and produced the subject, placing it in an easel.

"The color, style and materials are quite good. They've even aged it, probably with a hairdryer, microwave or something like that. An amateur wouldn't spot the flaws, but whoever produced it didn't expect a professional examination."

"Keep it for me and write up a report. We may need it in court and thanks."

Once inside Jennifer's car, Gamble called Stone. He answered on the second ring. "I need to see you," said Gamble. "You choose the place."

"Quincy Market, in the rotunda on the second floor. One o'clock. Come alone."

"I'd like to bring Jennifer."

"No one else."

"He's on the hook. Anxious too."

"He's not going to believe you if I go along."

"I know. I'll meet him alone. You can wait for me downstairs, but I want you in plain sight. It's important that he sees you. I want him to know I have a witness."

"I'd feel a lot better if you would wear a wire."

"I can't take the chance. Besides, if this goes as planned, it won't matter. Let's alert the detectives, shall we?"

Shortly before one, Jennifer and Gamble casually moved down the center of the food court. Jennifer wore a two-way wire to keep in contact with the detectives. The two men, once inside the building, separated and moved down the outer aisles, keeping in touch with her as they paralleled the pair's movements.

"If Stone's smart, he's been here for at least half an hour. By now, he's upstairs in the balcony, looking for us," said Gamble. "Keep walking and keep your pace the same as the crowd. When you reach the rotunda, find a seat and wait. I'm going ahead."

Reaching the circular eating area in the center of the building, he mounted the stairs to the balcony and found an empty space along the railing. A few minutes later, Stone joined him.

"You left the young lady downstairs."

"She's not a party to our conversation. I want her as a witness to our meeting."

"What's this all about?" asked Stone.

"I've got a proposition for you, one that should prove beneficial to both of us."

"Go on, I'm listening."

"The police are assembling quite a case against you and your friend."

"My information tells me they're more interested in you than me, my friend."

"Things have changed. If you read the papers yesterday, you would have learned that I was arrested at the airport, coming back from a quick trip to France, but I was released due to insufficient evidence."

"Business or pleasure? It's quite lovely there this time of the year. I hope to spend some time there very soon."

"Unfortunately it wasn't pleasure. We were pressed for time, but I did experience a trip on that wonderful high-speed train to Marseilles and then spent a few very interesting days in Avignon."

"This sounds intriguing. And did you take the obligatory photos to show the folks back home?"

"As a matter of fact, I did." Gamble reached into his coat pocket and pulled out an envelope. "You might want to look at these," he replied and waited as Stone opened the flap.

"As you can see, they're pictures of your home. I'm impressed. Wonderful restoration. Must have cost you a fortune."

"Why would you want pictures of my home? I already told you of its existence. Did you think I was lying?"

"Keep looking. The others are far more interesting."

Stone began flipping through the remaining pictures. "You bypassed the alarm and broke into my home. Haven't lost your touch, I see."

"It wasn't difficult." Gamble took the photos back and shuffled through them until he found the ones he wanted. "These two are particularly interesting. I took them in the barn on your property. You've got quite an impressive collection." He pointed to one of the photos. "They appear to be the same paintings you're trying to sell here. How can that be?"

"Save the sarcasm. What is it you want?"

"The stolen art scheme was brilliant, but you couldn't stop there. Why sell the original when you could sell forgeries? That way you could make a substantial profit on the same subject three or four times. No one could complain. After all, the transactions were illegal. Very nice."

"Get on with it."

"You're about to take on a new partner, some new blood to bring new ideas to the table."

"And who did you have in mind?"

"Why, me of course! I've got a vested interest in all this. I feel as though I've been associated with the whole scheme from the beginning. After all, I did the groundwork. You've been using my research all these years and I feel I'm entitled to some remuneration."

"And what figure did you have in mind?"

"I don't want to appear greedy. I think two million and a percentage of future profits would be about right."

"You've got to be crazy. I don't have that kind of money."

"Oh, come now, Stone. Let's not play games. Two million will hardly deplete your funds. I have complete faith in your resources. The quiet life of a wealthy English gentleman farmer has always been high on your list of priorities. That's why I'm sure you have quite a bit salted away for that rainy day we talked about. I'm a reasonable man. You'll need time to shift funds. I can wait. Shall we say, by Friday."

"You don't give me much time."

"It takes a few minutes to transfer money from one account to another. Which account you want to invade should be your only problem. Friday will give you plenty of time to make that decision. I'll give you my Swiss account number then."

"You still use the Swiss? Why not the islands?"

"A creature of habit. Besides, the Swiss are so precise. Always correct to the penny." Gamble shifted his stance. The muscles in his back were cramping. "Now that we're partners, so to speak, do you mind if I ask you a few questions?"

"I suppose not."

"When did you decide to delve into forgery?"

"In the early sixties. We were bored."

"You and Keegan? I wondered if you two remained together."

"Of course, I needed him. It was his network, you see. His relatives on his mother's side are French. They helped us from the beginning. We were wealthy by then, but there's only so much you can do; travel, investments, entertaining. We needed something to occupy our minds. After so many years of scheming and deception, it wasn't possible to relax."

"Whose idea was it?"

"Actually a nephew of Keegan's. An art student, quite good, I might add. He came to us with the idea. He and a friend demonstrated their talents and showed us several of their adaptations. They were perfect, right down to color and detail. They even had a process to age the canvas. It wouldn't pass the scrutiny of a museum or someone of your expertise, but could fool someone with no education or real appreciation of art. Our targets were those who wanted to hang something on the wall and brag as to its cost. You'd be surprised how many people want to be fooled."

"And the originals?"

"We sold some of them too, after we made several copies, of course. You've seen the studio. It's quite elaborate. Plenty of light, climate controlled, lavish living quarters. Our artists are content and quite wealthy, I might add."

"Has anyone tried to cash in on this?"

"You mean threaten to go to the police? Why? They'd have to give back the money and face a possible jail sentence. And blackmail! Out of the question. My people are well paid." Stone started to walk away.

"What happened to my deal with the police?"

"This is a much better arrangement. I'll expect your call." Gamble watched the man descend the stairs and disappear into the crowd. His reaction to the meeting was mixed. He had to hand it to Stone. The man knew how to keep things close to his vest. Cool as ever.

He waited a few minutes and joined Jennifer on the ground floor. She signaled the detectives that they were ready to leave as they stepped out into the warm spring air.

"Let's walk," said Gamble as they passed Faneuil Hall.

"Every time I pass this building, I try to focus on what it represents: freedom and all that goes with it. It helps put things in perspective. I spent most of my life dealing with the ruthless and unethical, but most of the world is good. At least, I hope so. Otherwise, why bother?"

"Come on." Jennifer took his arm. "Let's go home. Now the hardest part begins, the waiting."

Conlon, along with several customs agents, waited for the cargo to be unloaded from the Air France flight from Paris. They searched several large crates, resealed and released them to the pickup area, then watched three men load them into a plain green van. Two unmarked police vehicles followed at a discreet distance as it proceeded through the Callahan Tunnel and worked its way around the construction traffic and parked on the alley behind the Newbury Street gallery.

The police waited patiently until everything was unloaded before they made their move. Conlon, a customs agent, and two uniforms approached the front while a similar team waited at the service entrance. Inside, they found Tyler in his office, checking invoices against order sheets.

Conlon identified himself while the others slipped in the back door. "Mr. Tyler, you're under arrest for customs violations, grand theft and conspiracy to commit murder."

"Hey, take it easy. I don't know what you're talking about."

"We followed your van from the airport. The crates were inspected before they cleared customs and we found some very interesting pieces of art."

"This is an art gallery. What did you expect?"

"Exactly what were looking for. Stolen art and forgeries. Paintings that don't appear on the manifest for starters." He pulled a warrant from his pocket. "And this allows us to search the premises. Who knows what we'll find? Then, there's the little charge of murder, two counts."

"I'm only the manager. I do what I'm told and don't know anything about murder. I didn't work here then."

"You can explain all that downtown." He turned to an officer. "Read him his rights and take him in while we have a look around. Oh, before you go, open the safe."

The manager twisted the dials and stepped away.

Conlon pulled on his latex gloves and removed several packets of bills, all neatly wrapped, on the floor. "You better get a good attorney."

Chapter Seventeen

Stone was in a quandary. He was being blackmailed, but how to handle Coulhoon was beyond his capabilities. Greed, simple greed got him in this mess, and he had no one but himself to blame. As he waited in his hotel room, he examined all the possibilities. Only one could solve his problem. He was about to pour himself a drink when Keegan arrived.

"We have another problem," said Stone. "Mr. Coulhoon has decided we owe him a percentage of our profits."

"What's his angle?"

"He wants two million dollars. He feels we used his research and deserves compensation. He also wants a percentage of future earnings. In other words, he wants to become a silent partner."

"What's your take on it?"

"I think he's serious about the money, but I think we can compromise on the amount."

"And we're supposed to think this guy can be bought? I don't think so. That kind of guy, he doesn't change. It's either right or wrong. Nothin' in the middle."

"Then how do we solve this problem?"

"We'll have to persuade him that a life of crime is not for him. Let me deal with it, maybe scare him, rough him up. 'Course, I got to talk to our partners. We can't do nothin' without them."

"I leave it in your capable hands, but I don't ever want to know the details."

"If he calls, stall him. Tell him you've got to get with your pals and you'll get back to him." Keegan opened the door. "I'll keep in touch. Relax. You don't look too good."

Once outside, Keegan ducked into a doorway and used his phone. "Stone's in bad shape. Coulhoon gave him some cock-and-bull story about wanting to become a partner. Says we owe it to him. I said he can't be trusted and that I'd take care of it."

"Do you think we could be looking at the wrong guy for these killings?" Jennifer and Conlon were sitting on the front steps of her building. It was a beautiful spring night and they were enjoying the fresh evening breeze.

"Why? Do you have someone else in mind?" he asked.

"Maybe we're so hung up on Harrington, we can't see beyond him. Who else would benefit from Stone's elimination and Gamble's for that matter?"

Both remained silent, using the time to think.

"Are you thinking what I'm thinking?" he asked.

"There's only one other person and we don't have a clue where he is."

Conlon stood up. "Gamble could be in danger. We

could have been chasing the wrong guy all along. Atkins and Klein are staked out at Gamble's place, but this guy is slippery. I'll check with them, but I'm going to take a look myself."

"Not without me."

Gamble settled in a tan leather chair, his back to the opened French doors leading to his tiny brick patio. With a cup of coffee in one hand and a pen in the other, he began reviewing his notes for the next day's lecture. They had decided to let Stone stew for twenty-four hours.

Suddenly, he heard the sound of rubber scrunching against brick. Instinctively, he placed the cup aside and reached for the consoling touch of cold steel from a small but powerful revolver concealed behind the flattened red pillow tucked under his left elbow. His company was not unexpected.

He heard the sound again. Pretending to continue reading, he jotted down imaginary ideas in the margin and waited. "You never were a cautious man," he said, quietly waiting for his visitor to make his presence officially known.

"You always did have a great sense of hearing. No one could enter a room without you knowing it." The figure moved into the light, gun in hand, and stopped a few feet from the chair.

"Everyone thinks the Major killed René but he doesn't have the stomach for it."

Gamble gripped the gun handle a little tighter. "I wasn't sure you were still alive until a few days ago."

"I'm not so easy to kill." The Corporal, Sean Keegan, moved closer into the light. A small man, still lean and trim, he was losing his hair, but the face was still gaunt. His small dark eyes darted from side to side behind thin-rimmed glasses, just as they did fifty years ago. He still looked like a ferret. Gamble recognized him right away.

"I imagine you've eliminated Stone, weak link and all."

"The Major will meet with an untimely death, as you educated guys would say. He's next on my list. No one will find him, at least for awhile. The cops will think he got nervous and slipped town. In a way, he will, wouldn't you say?"

"You've been in on it from the beginning, I gather."

"Always loved the way you talked. Almost English, Professor. I used to call you that, remember?"

"It escaped my memory, but, yes, I do recall it now." Gamble shifted his weight slightly for balance, ready to make a quick move if the opportunity presented itself. "Tell me, how does this whole operation work, if you don't mind telling me."

He found a ladderback chair, settled in, and seemed to relax a little. "I think you might enjoy this story. The Major and me, we planned it one rainy afternoon while you were slaving away in the cellar. I never could understand why you worked down there."

"It was cool and dry. Temperature and atmosphere are important factors in preserving works of art."

"That place gave me the creeps. Anyway, I digress. How do you like them words? I picked them up from the Major."

"I'm sure he's pleased that he helped further your education."

"The Major wanted to ask you if you wanted in, but I told him you wouldn't go for it."

"You were right."

"I asked him what he thought about stealing the stuff. He knew I'd been dealing on the black market and thought it would work. I had family in Paris, so I got in touch with a few guys, who got in touch with a few guys, you know how that goes and we set it up."

"Fascinating, but why include the Major? It sounds as though you could handle the whole thing yourself."

"He was in charge and it would have been hard to hide things from him and he had contacts in high places. A couple of guys in London, who, for a piece of the action were willing to play along. Real high-class types. Goes to show ya, everybody likes to chase the buck. Besides, if I did it on my own, he'd have figured it out. I couldn't take the chance."

"Did the Major tell you I had a copy of the inventory?"

"Yeah, we thought it might be a problem, but we had it so good for so many years, I guess we got careless."

Suddenly, the phone rang. "Answer it," he ordered. "And no funny stuff."

Gamble picked it up on the third ring.

"Gamble, it's Jennifer. Just checking in."

"I'm working on my lecture notes." Gamble watched Keegan, his face a blank.

"Don't do nothin' stupid," Keegan whispered.

"Have you called Stone yet?"

"No, later on."

"Call me when you make contact."

"Good idea. I'll call you then." He placed the phone face down on the receiver.

"Very nice, Professor, but then you were always the cool one."

"You haven't finished your story."

"You really want to know the rest?"

"I'm always interested in a good tale. And must you wave that gun around? I assure you, I'm not about to be a hero. I'm much too old for that."

"I'm no chicken, myself, but I'm still a good shot."

He lowered the gun slightly, but still pointed at Gamble. "The Major planned most of it. He made a copy of everything at night and arranged for a fence. I found a place to stash the stuff and supplied the men and the trucks."

"Who arranged the disappearance?"

"I did. We pushed the jeep into the river. It took the cops weeks to find it. We holed up in a fleabag hotel while my guys took the stuff from the bank. I still had a key and it was easy for them to clean the place out in one night. It was real nice for the Army to crate everything for us. They loaded it on a couple of trucks and stashed it in a warehouse in Marseilles, owned by a cousin of mine. We left it there for a few months until everything cooled down."

"You assumed new identities."

"Got phony passports, papers, the works. The Major found a place in the country, Avignon, where the Romans built their aqueducts. No one thought to look for us there. The Major, he's smart, but I guess you know all this by now."

"Let me try and guess what happened next," replied Gamble. "You waited awhile; I'd say a couple of years. Then you began selling bit by bit to private collectors, ones who wouldn't question where the paintings came from. Then, an occasional piece on the open market, nothing controversial, but good. I tried to keep track, but auctioneers and gallery owners aren't very helpful."

"We had a good thing going. Everybody got his cut; nobody got greedy, until that stupid André. I told the Major he couldn't be trusted, but he wouldn't listen. The little jerk said he had someone interested in the painting. Only the deal fell through, so he put them in the window."

"Is that when you decided to kill him?"

"He panicked when you and that nosy lawyer began asking questions."

"When I saw the paintings the first time, they were real, but you must have switched them because the next time, I saw the forgeries."

"We started making the copies a few years ago. Never to dealers, they would have caught on. We pawned them off on the easy marks. Why sell the real thing when you could make millions on phony stuff? Worked like a charm."

"And the Major?"

"He didn't like the fakes at first, but when we started making all that money, he went along. But now, with you nosing around, well, he's got to go. He can't handle the pressure and wants to pay you off, but we know that won't work."

"We? You're referring to your new partner, Tim Harrington?"

"No, he don't like all the publicity. I use my nephew. He's my right-hand man. I'm too old for all this killing."

"You're the one who's been following Jennifer and me."

"Had to keep an eye on you."

"And the Major?"

"The same for him. He was getting too nervous."

"Why the girl, Miss Lassiter?"

"She found out about everything and tried to blackmail us. Can you believe it? She invited me to her apartment so we could make a deal. She must have been crazy. She really thought she could hold me up. It wasn't the money, 'cause she didn't ask for all that much; it was the whole idea that she thought she could pull it off. I couldn't let her get away with it."

"So, you killed her."

"Yeah, I did. I almost felt sorry after I did it, but I had no choice."

"That jacket you have on. You were wearing it the night the girl was killed. The police have fibers that I'm sure will match it perfectly."

"Thanks for the tip. I'll get rid of it."

"And now, I suppose it's my turn."

"Sorry, Professor. Always liked you. You're a stand-up guy, but I got to protect myself. I still got a few more good years left and I don't want to spend them looking over my shoulder. You really didn't think I'd go for the idea that you could change sides. That would never happen. You're too straight."

"How does Timmy Harrington fit into all this?"

"Timmy's dad and I go way back. When we decided to make Boston one of our outlets, I contacted him. I needed protection. He needed a new way to get money, drugs, and some guns out of the country. We get along just fine, but if he knew it was me knocking off these people, I'd be dead myself."

"Why did you go to Jennifer's apartment?"

"The Major thought she might have a copy of your notes, you being so friendly with her. She's a little young for you, isn't she?"

"Don't be idiotic."

Suddenly, they heard a car door close.

"Must be your neighbors coming home," said Keegan. "We'll wait until they go inside, then you and me, we're gonna take a little ride." He backed away to the terrace door.

"Sorry to put a crimp in your plans." Conlon and his two detectives with their guns drawn appeared in the doorway behind him. "Put your gun down and step back."

Keegan slowly dropped to his knees and set the gun

on the floor. He looked at Gamble as he stood up and backed away.

"You were always smart, always smart. How did you manage this?"

Suddenly, Jennifer burst through the door.

"I thought I told you to wait outside."

"You didn't expect me to stay there all night, did you?" she huffed.

"I consider myself lucky you waited this long," said Conlon.

"How on earth did you get here?" asked Gamble.

"We were having dinner and talking about the case," said Jennifer. "It suddenly dawned on me that maybe we were looking in the wrong direction. We had everyone under suspicion, everyone but one. We all thought Harrington was our man. We wanted it to be him. This obsession with him put blinders on us. Then I started thinking. Who else would benefit from DeLacroix's death and yours, Gamble? Who had the most to gain? It had to be Keegan. There wasn't anyone else."

"Then, I thought about our phone conversation. You never prepare notes. You've given that lecture so many times; you know it in your sleep. Something had to be wrong."

Conlon continued. "I patched through to Atkins. He and Klein have been watching your place for the last three nights. They mentioned that the lights were still on in your apartment. They thought it was strange because you have been going to bed at eleven every night, like clockwork. We put two and two together and decided you were in trouble. They were outside on the terrace the whole time, listening to every word."

"I hope this will get me off the hook with Interpol and everyone else," said Gamble.

"I'll clear it with everyone in the morning. Interpol

will have their hands full unraveling the whole art deal and the DA's office can deal with the murders. I'm sure the fingerprints on the parking stub will match Keegan's or the kid and the jacket fibers should clinch the Lassiter girl's murder. We'll have to work on the DeLacroix case, but if the bullets from both murders came from his gun, I don't think we'll have a problem. Now, let's get him downtown. He'll make the Chief's day."

"What about Stone?" asked Gamble.

"We're looking for him now. Gamble says he's willing to cooperate."

The celebration was over. Jennifer and Conlon stood on the sidewalk in front of her father's house and watched the cab with Gamble and Marko, safely inside, drive away. "Let's walk," said Jennifer. "It's a beautiful night." She took his arm as they started down the hill. "Now that we've got Stone's deposition and willingness to testify, I doubt Sean Keegan will ever spend another day on the outside. It won't be so easy with Harrington. He knows how to cover his tracks and has enough money to hire the best lawyers in town. We might not be able to make anything stick."

"Some day he'll make one big mistake." They walked for a while in silence, enjoying a few peaceful minutes in what was usually a chaotic life for two busy people.

"What kind of deal did you make with Stone?"

"He gets immunity for his part in the whole scheme. After all, he was never a part of the murders. I think he would have done a disappearing act if he knew Keegan was behind it. Interpol will shut down his forgery scheme and confiscate what originals are left and of course, he'll have to give up his Swiss bank accounts."

"All of them?"

"You know better than that. I'm sure he'll continue living a very comfortable life."

"What about his villa in France?"

"That's up to the French government, but he'll find a way to hold on to it. After all, he supports the whole village."

"I hope Gamble and Marko have decided to retire permanently. I'm not sure I can take another case that involves him."

"He does make life interesting." Jennifer stopped to organize her words before continuing. "Speaking of changes in lifestyles, what would you think if I told you I was considering going back to the DA's office?"

"It doesn't surprise me."

"Why not?"

"You're a great defense attorney, my love, but your heart has always been on the other side. What brought this on?"

"I had a chat with Mancuso. He wants me back."

"He's always wanted you back. Why now?"

"He's going to make a run for Attorney General."

"He's got a great chance to win. Who better knows how the system works? What's his offer?"

"I come back, he appoints me successor until the next election. I've got two years to smooth out the rough edges and make nice with everyone."

"You're going to make some powerful enemies."

"I can deal with them."

"Speaking of changes, your father asked me when we were going to set the date. I told him we were thinking about it."

"Good answer. Oh, I almost forgot." She reached

into her bag and pulled out a postcard. "From Stone. It's a picture of the Vienna Opera House."

Conlon took the postcard and turned it over. "Having a wonderful time."

"I'm sure he is."